DEVOURING
L I G H T

DEVOURING
L I G H T

by *J.M. Ney-Grimm*

Wild
Unicorn

ISBN-13: 978-0615973135
ISBN-10: 0615973132

Designed by JMNG

Cover art:

"Woman in a White Dress"
by Irina Gromovataya / Dreamstime.com

"Sun Emits a Solstice CME"
from NASA Goddard Space Flight Center

"Starry Night" by Silvertiger / Dreamstime

For Dad,
because of the love of astronomy
he instilled in me

And with thanks to D.J.G.
for noticing
all the cool bits

Devouring Light is fantasy,
but its inspiration lies in science

The Celestial Spheres of Sol's Demesne

Sol and each of Sol's planets – through its guardian – generates a celestial sphere.

Each guardian tends that one heavenly body and its sphere, performs certain tasks for his or her fellow guardians, and – sometimes – grants the prayers of Earth's children.

Mercurio Veloxus Ludificor, guardian of Mercury, carries messages between the spheres.

Sol rules over all of them.

First Sphere
The Sun tended by Sol

Second Sphere
Mercury tended by Mercurio

Third Sphere
Venus tended by Star

Fourth Sphere
Main Ellipse
Earth tended by Gaia

Dependent Ellipse
The Moon tended by Artemis Diana

Fifth Sphere

INNER ELLIPSE

Mars tended by Ares

OUTER ELLIPSE

The Asteroids tended by Plurima

Ceres tended by Ceres

Sixth Sphere

Jupiter tended by Basileus

Seventh Sphere

INNER ELLIPSE

Saturn tended by Saturnus

MIDDLE ELLIPSE

Uranus tended by Ouranos

OUTER ELLIPSE

Neptune tended by Neptunus Equester

Eighth Sphere

The Zodiac Perspective inhabited by the
Constellations

Ninth Sphere

Pluto tended by Haden

The Ecclesiast's Voice

These are the admonishments from mortal to immortal.
Save me. Preserve me. Send me fortune fair.

Such are the pleas from man or woman
to god and goddess in their spheres.

Chill Haden, hold your line. Let Pluto's revolutions protect
the living from the dead. Keep the darkness always far from me.
Keep the brilliance always bright.

Mighty Draco, what of you? A constellation like your neighbors,
you map the psyche of my soul. Will I be the salamander,
ever burning bright – breathing wisdom from my fires,
birthing life from my might? Or will I be the dragon
with destruction in my wake?

Timekeeping Mercurio, be steady in your beat. Mark the seasons
of my planting. Mark the seasons of my heart. But falter
never ever, lest my darkness rule my light.

My core, my essence, my beginning and my end.
Great Sol, the progenitor. Great Sol, my friend. Nurture me,
your child, spawn of star dust and of space. Stoke your furnace,
stoke your heart. Let earth's day emerge from night.
Keep the balance. Keep my life. Let me live and live again.

Admonishment, plea, and prayer:
pull me always from devouring night.

— inscribed on the Arduvallean Stone,
fourth celestial sphere

DEVOURING
LIGHT

The dark enfolded him, cool, almost palpable.

How long had he sat here with the lanterns doused?

Sensing the otherness of his realm in a way that only sightless perception permitted, his place of earth and stone and the slow drip of water across centuries. Feeling the imprint of a fossilized leaf, the pulsing breath of blind creatures, the seeping creep of moisture. Hearing the clear echo of a drop of water hitting an underground pool in the distance.

Haden shifted his haunches, easing their soreness where the granite of his lonely throne pressed.

The dark comforted him with its familiarity.

Was it merely yesterday? Or a millennium? Or a galactic year – the patient span of time in which Sol would circle the vast spiral of the Milky Way – since Haden had ordered the fires extinguished and sought this seat, the private bench sequestered in a narrow corner?

In his mind's eye, he could see the banquet hall with its elaborate divans, its moving flambeaus, its warmth and light.

His wife had cared to order it so, bright with the flames, the choice viands, and the music of the lyre players. Her lips blushed rose, moist with the juice of the fruit from which her fingers plucked the pips. How sweet had it tasted, the nectar of the pomegranate? Gliding across her tongue and down her slender throat. Had its savor balanced the price she paid?

The dark was friendlier to him than these memories.

Their vivid happiness oppressed him. Better to contemplate the cool scents of rock and loam and water. From the earth, all wealth was born. *I am the giver of bounty, the root of the harvest.*

Had Proserpina thought so?

He lifted his shoulders, let them settle again. The weight of his tunic, woven of heavy gold threads, pressed against his collar bones, dragged over his knees, and formed a pillow of folds on his instep. His toga, of thick wool, spared him the chill in this buried march. Spared him bruises when he shifted incautiously.

He missed her. His wife.

Had the summer passed? The warm months upon Gaia's breast when Proserpina wandered sunlit meadows and sun-dappled groves? While he lurked below in darkness, in stillness.

She brought summer with her, when she returned. And yet . . . her winter months were here at his side. Not here on this solitary throne, but here below as Queen of the Underworld, upon her royal bench in the shadow-hung throne room.

I am the darkness, the quietus, the halt at the end. The passing from life into death. I am content.

What was this yearning for brightness that stirred in his core?

I eschew it.

Crack! The two snaky tails snapped silver lightning past Mercurio's nose.

He jumped and laughed.

"Have a care there, Draco. Who would trust a thief without comeliness? You'll bankrupt me faster than a con man!"

The hissing roar of Draco's voice replied,

"Younger cousin, 'tis you who sought me." And his tails cracked again, powerful, muscular, scaled in cold burning silver stars.

Mercurio dodged, tripped on the rumpled midnight folds of sky underfoot, barked his shins against a star remnant fixed inconveniently in midair, and swore.

"Cronos! You could tidy your lair!"

If lair were the proper term for this sky refuge, perched in the eighth celestial sphere, belted by the zodiac and roamed by constellations.

Near and far were strangely confused, as were matter and space. The velvet dusk of the cosmos varied inconsistently in the eighth sphere, firm as flooring in one spot, yielding as a tent in another, and open the way it looked in yet another.

How was an immortal to place his feet? Or not – as caprice might have it – while eluding the thrashing coils of a curmudgeonly dragon? Thank Vulcanus for his sandals and their wings.

The view was spectacular though!

The constellations danced and sang and soared through the living night. Graceful Cygnus and lumbering Ursa Major nearby, the fiery Phoenix far along the mighty curve of the sphere. A veritable zoo. Perfect for the spectacle he planned.

"C'mon Draco! I'll even get Andromeda to play the damsel in distress. You'll love it."

Draco loomed large, reptilian, and uncooperative in the center of his refuge. His tails cracked a third time, emphasizing his displeasure.

"Would she let me devour her, younger cousin?" he asked, a sly note edging his harsh tones.

Mercurio slipped on a spill of star dust, swallowed his further complaint, and sprang upward. If there were any real upward in the sphere. But standing – or pacing – amidst its inconsistencies was a pain. Might as well spread his sandal wings. He maneuvered away from Draco's twitching tails toward the constellation's face.

Draco yawned.

A miasma of burning cold belched from his gullet.

Ah! Not directly in front then. Right.

Mercurio retreated to the side. "What if I fetched you a Gaian maiden? For afterward," he added. Spurting blood was *not* the spectacle he had in mind.

"Too bland," returned Draco. "And Auntie Guy would never let you anyway."

Now *that* was true. Gaia was . . . protective. What else could Mercurio offer in persuasion? "I could get Juno to stage a race to the Table and back." The dragon would like stretching his wings, wouldn't he?

Draco snickered, and Mercurio shuddered. A blast furnace opening its maw, that's what it sounded like, despite its chill.

"I don't need your blandishments to coax Juno. I've blandishments of my own."

Also true. But surely Mercurio possessed something Draco wanted. "Name your price!" he blurted. Uh, oh. That was a mistake. Cronos only knew what the dragon might come up with. And once he settled on something, he wouldn't take anything else.

Draco's left tail twitched, and Mercurio jerked backward, anticipating another cracking lash. But Draco was settling, coiling in on himself, calming. He tilted the dark lamps of eyes, fringed by their silver tendrils, up toward his visitor. His long lipless mouth twitched. "Would you lend me your sandals?"

What? Mercurio wrinkled his brow. "You have your own wings. Why d'you want mine?"

Draco's voice grew mild. "Is not flight powered by thought different from that achieved via muscular effort? I'm curious."

Oh. Was Draco serious? Well . . . Mercurio had lent his footwear once before. And how well had that worked? Not very. "Um."

"Never mind." Odd that Draco's voice could

sound airy, despite its grating undertones. "They'd never go over my claws anyway." The dragon lifted his great fore paw, extending its scythe-sharp talons, then allowing them to retract as he set it down again.

"Um."

"Feline got your tongue, god of eloquence?"

"I thought you'd say yes. That you'd want to participate, to please Sol. It's his twenty-fifth."

"Ah, yes, the grand dance of our light, swinging through the vast dark for two hundred and fifty million Gaian years each circuit. 'Tis a worthy anniversary, the twenty-fifth." Draco's eyes were almost closed. "Worthy of spectacle, worthy of celebration, worthy of me."

"Then you'll do it? You'll promise?"

Draco's eyes opened. "No. Wild power never promises, younger cousin. It cannot be so chained."

"You have personal will, elder cousin." There. That acerbic tone was just right. Would Draco be swayed?

The dragon yawned, belching another chilling mist. Mercurio backed further, midair, and felt the whisper of velvet against his shoulders. He'd reached the perimeter of Draco's refuge.

"Does Chalcedonie speak to you?" murmured Draco.

Once more Mercurio found himself bereft of words. The spirit of the Milky Way herself? Not even "um" emerged this time.

"Would she open her fires for you?"

Mercurio descended abruptly, his knees buckling slightly upon landing. This piece of floor was solid. He recovered his balance, threaded his thumbs through either side of his belt, and stood tall.

"No. No, she doesn't. I'll take my leave." Cronos, that sounded pompous. But there were limits! He'd never even met Chalcedonie Galaxias, let alone achieved intimacy with her.

Draco's eyes closed again. "Thought you lacked my coin," he muttered. "Come back, if you gain it, though I doubt you will."

But Mercurio was winging his way home. Draco had wanted to say no. *I'll just have to find a way to* make *him perform.* Diplomacy wasn't the answer.

To mere eyes, the zodiac's sun shone unremarkably within the eighth sphere, one star among a vast field of others, its pivot point too distant from the eighth's great orbit. But when Draco closed or ignored his eyes, ah, then Sol's power reigned supreme. A blazing weighty force anchoring everything from Mercurio's quickened race through Haden's ponderous tread to the comets' ballet in the far Oort Cloud.

"It is time," hissed Draco to himself.

Then he lingered, watching Mercurio's soaring figure dwindle, shrinking with distance against the midnight blue starfield, then fading in the translation from one sphere to the next.

So Mercurio honored Sol even now, after the passage of six and a quarter billion Gaian years. Draco snickered, feeling the frost of his breath cooling his face, tasting ice. So too did Draco honor Sol, even now. But no elder cousin turned on a drachma, not even for Sol, let alone at the bidding of a fledgling planetary upstart.

Sol would have his celebration, oh yes. A spectacle more extravagant than anything young Mercurio dreamed up.

Draco stirred his coils, uncurling, unfurling, stretching in sinuous indulgence.

Yes, it was time.

He sprang from his crouch, colossal wings spread to collect power and thundering down to lift him. Draco soared out from his lair, that pocket within the cosmos that was his. It dwindled behind him, then faded in the distance. Not inward to seven, then six, but outward to nine. Not brightward in Mercurio's wake, but nightward, into Haden's dark sphere.

He arrived in the throne room, its rock-bound shadows darker than the inviting skies of home, more chill than the living shadow between the stars. Draco suppressed a shudder and furled his wings, tucking them back along his flanks. The dark pressed unrelenting, but a faint phosphorescence outlined corners, the unlit iron branches of flambeaus, and the paired thrones. The room was empty.

Draco sighed, contracted yet more, and reversed his length to move toward the small opening at his tail. Moping in the catacombs yet again, was Haden? Well, Draco would find him there, despite Haden's desire for seclusion. Perhaps his proposed project would stir the king of the infernal abyss out of his melancholy.

Draco clamped his wings tighter and pulled his limbs inward, becoming serpent, slithering through the rocky narrows, down and down.

"Depart, ophidian," breathed the chill air.

Ah, the leftmost tunnel. Draco maneuvered and approached his dour cousin.

"Does Nyx succor you, cousin?" It was hard to expand his dragon lungs enough to generate voice. His question whispered along the tunnel to where

Haden sat, unmoving.

"I hold no audience without my queen."

So. Haden would be difficult. "Yet I approach."

Silence.

Draco repeated himself. "I approach, cousin."

"Your scent repels me, ophidian."

"So it is meant to do." Draco sniffed. "Nevertheless. I approach."

Now he could see Haden, still and upright on a meager bench against the rough rock of the tunnel where it bent sharply, illuminated only by hints of phosphor on surfaces and edges. The king's face held no expression, his eyes hidden by the shadows. Faint glimmers hinted the metallic sheen of his long robes. Utter blackness wrapped his toga. He spoke again. "It is said that Chaos precedes Night."

"So it is said," answered Draco. "And it is said again that between Chaos and Night came another, a darker dark, a more violent chaos. Do you know it?"

"I have heard of such." Did Haden's tone grow distant?

"And if I confirmed it?"

"You are old, cousin. Are you so old as that?" A faint tinge of warmth in Haden's words?

"Yesss," Draco's tongue hissed the affirmation. "Oh, yesss. I am old and older, star dust among novae, power in the primordial slurry. I am old."

"And this confirmation?"

"On Chalcedonie's left hand it rests, hidden in the folds of her gown, forgotten amidst the honors of her brilliances. Gravity beyond gravity, straightness bent to convolution, darkness turned to absence."

"Then fetch it to me, elder cousin."

"Ah!" He'd piqued Haden's interest, as he'd hoped. "There lies the difficulty. This dragon of the cosmos overmatches me."

Silence again, but a listening silence.

"But not you," concluded Draco.

"Has it a name, this being between Chaos and Nyx? A pedigree?" Haden leaned forward. Phosphorescence reached his eyes, gleaming, not flat.

Draco felt his own lips draw back in a nasty smile. "Oh, many names, cousin, many. Teleio mauro. Perfectum nigra. Gravissimum gravitatum. But only one pedigree. Absolute weight."

"And I may fetch it? Truly?"

"Would you wish me tell you how?"

A third silence, a living silence, a silence of yes.

Mercurio sighed as he materialized within the portal hall of the second sphere. It felt good to be home.

On generous walls and a high ceiling, great bronze gears revolved around their spindles, turning smaller gears and crankshafts, pushing the needles on dials and recording gauges. Faint clicks attended their procession. The air was gently warm, pleasant after the chill of traversing the more distant spheres. And it smelled right: faintly cinnamony and woody.

As Mercurio bent to loosen his sandal straps, a cat lounged out from beneath the marble-topped console table in the center of the space and twined around his ankles. Mercurio paused to stroke the creature's nudging head.

"All well here, Vigilem?"

Clockwork, like the hall in which they stood, Vigilem looked like petting him would not be satisfying: scaled in electrum stars, rather than pelted; rigid-bodied; an automaton. But his scales were pliable and warm. His movement possessed the fluidity of a living organism. And he purred.

"Yesss, clock winder. Each gear meshes with its neighbor, each shaft transfers the requisite force, and the sphere holds its proper configuration entire."

Why did Mercurio sense the cat was laughing? Mercurio always asked when he'd been away. Even though Vigilem would have summoned him if something went wrong in his absence.

"And?" queried Mercurio.

"Prrrrr," answered Vigilem, and stalked away toward the *calces maximus*, the gear connected to the vast orbital sphere.

Mercurio shrugged and pulled his sandals off, shoving them under the console table. He'd find out what it was all about soon enough. In the meantime . . . what was this?

The scent of apricots rose from a ewer on a tray – both electrum – on the console. Mercurio poured a generous measure into the accompanying goblet and swigged. Tingling sweetness filled his mouth. Ah, yes. His favorite flavor. Bless Hebe for her choice. Haden might prefer pomegranate, but Mercurio did not. He frowned.

Haden.

That was where all the repeated noes were leading him.

Draco had said no. (To the monster drama.)

Before Draco, Saturnus had said no. (To the clown charade.)

And before Saturnus, Star had said it. (To the lady-on-a-prancing-horse act.) Or, rather, she said, "Goodness, dear boy, that's so clichéd! No!"

Mercurio downed the rest of the nectar, replaced the goblet on the tray, and slouched over to the gauge beside the *calces maximus*.

A long scroll of parchment unfurled from the moving stylus to pile on the diamond-textured bronze floor. Mercurio picked up the end of the scroll, studying the record. The line of ink left by the stylus traced the long curves normal to his planet's orbit, currently half a degree north of the ecliptic, transiting Sol. Mercurio's eyes followed the trace all the way to the drum over which the parchment draped.

Yes, yes, yes . . . what?

Not a bobble, no. The line was smooth. But a speck next to it. That made no sense at all.

"Vigilem!"

The cat materialized almost under Mercurio's bare feet. His whiskers tickled Mercurio's toes. "Just a meteor, pendulum mover." Vigilem sniffed. "Or perhaps a comet passing through."

"Which?" The two were quite different, and Vigilem knew it. Why the ambiguity?

"A wanderer, then. A hobo. A vagabond." And he slunk off.

Something unfamiliar then. A one-of-a-kind celestial body floating through the solar system. Hmm.

Mercurio checked the next in the array of

monitoring devices, the rotation transcript. Same speck. Planetary magnetosphere? Speck. Coronal disturbances and solar flares? Speck. He was detecting a trend here. And Vigilem was being coy. Fine.

Mercurio headed for the nearer archway out of the hall, shedding his tunic as he stepped into the corridor beyond. *I'll bathe and catch a nap before I start for the ninth sphere.*

The thing was . . . why would Haden say yes when everyone else was saying no?

Because this was a different sort of request? Because darkness was Haden's love? Because all he knew was enduring disapproval? Because Mercurio's idea expressed the heart of Haden's essence?

Maybe. Or maybe he should have a back-up plan. Or maybe . . . he shouldn't ask it at all.

Gaia would judge that he was provoking Haden's worst nature. He could imagine the shadow crossing her face, her earth eclipsed by the moon indeed. Not a pretty sight. He'd quite liked it when she'd beamed at him during the last planetary conclave. There on her couch, nibbling grapes from one dainty hand, and nominating him – *him* – as the master of ceremonies, while the other seven planetaries looked on.

"We've done dark and dramatic. Three times," she pronounced, glancing at Haden across the circle of the dais. "Shining and ecstatic, twice." Her gaze at Star was kinder. "Quirky, once." That went to the one non-planetary present – Plurima. "Dignified, five times!" A sidelong acknowledgment to Basileus. "And every other kind of variation on joy and remembrance. I think it's time we apply to a more youthful point of view."

And she'd persuaded them.

He, Mercurio Veloxus Ludificor, would plan and conduct the festivities for Sol's twenty-fifth galactic anniversary of his birth. Even mighty Basileus had concurred, nodding judiciously. But best of all had been Gaia's private words to him after the others had gone.

He'd dithered a bit, worrying that Ares would deem his offering too tame, or Neptunus Equester, not horsey enough or insufficiently wet.

What an idiot he was! Speaking of wet, how about wet-behind-the-ears wet!

But Gaia's approval felt good.

"Just please yourself, 'Curio. Honestly. The others all did. Why shouldn't you? That was rather my point in nominating you." She smiled. "I want fun. I want young. I want frivolous. You'll deliver just that."

And he refused to let her down, devour it!

Sunlight from his conservatory shone through a

series of openings in the wall, reflecting bright on the corridor's metallic floor. Mercurio leaned through the arcade, arm slung around a column, eyes closed, to enjoy Sol's warmth.

The ambrosia trees were blooming, their spicy floral fragrance drifting into the passage. *Mmm.* Mercurio inhaled, then opened his eyes. The plantings resembled a jungle more than a garden, trees flooded with undergrowth and clambered over by vines. They hid the shape and extent of the space entirely, but Mercurio could hear the trickle of the central fountain even though he couldn't see it. Light poured through the crystal dome above, too intense for mortal eyes, should any stray here. Mercurio could discern Sol's outline, barely, the source of the cataract of radiance.

Vigilem reappeared to brush against Mercurio's calves. "Prrrr!" He enjoyed Sol's proximity too.

"C'mon, 'Gilem! Give! What do you know that you're not telling me?"

The cat disappeared into the greenery.

Mercurio walked on to the archway into his bedchamber and through it, tunic and loin brief casually slung in one hand. The gas lamps there were dim, barely lit, and the change from brilliance to abrupt shadow blinded him. Then his eyes adjusted.

Oh, ho, ho! So this was the celestial wanderer.

Nice. Very nice.

Asleep atop the cinnamon draperies of his couch, she wore the traditional peplos, the long feminine tunic. But so translucent was its cream silk that her limbs seemed almost unclothed.

His eyes roamed, drinking in her glory: curve of calf and hip and breast. Dusky hair bound up on her head with gold ribands, framing curve of jaw, cheek, and brow. From across the room, Mercurio's hand reached.

She was lovely.

He drew closer to the couch, dropping his garments somewhere en route. Haden could wait. This was worth savoring. In exquisite and lingering detail. He knelt. And her eyes opened languidly. Dark like her hair.

"Who are you?" she murmured. "Why do you loiter in my chamber?"

"To worship you, my charming hetaera."

The sleep left her face, a slight frown lowering her brows. She sat up. "Then don't, please. I would be alone. Be gone."

He didn't move. Did she really intend to spurn him? Here in *his* bedchamber?

She scooted to the far end of his couch, placing her feet on the floor, carpeted in here with decorative amber matting. Confusion was growing in her expression, displacing her irritation. She looked him full in the face, glanced down, blushed at his nakedness, and hurriedly returned her gaze to his face.

"You make a strange cupbearer, unclad and uncouth. Who named you as mine? They have something to answer for!"

"I name myself." He smiled at her. Perhaps a little enticement would do the trick. "Mercurio. Bearing cups for your bath, cups for your refreshment. A cup for your pleasure." He stretched toward her, starting to trace a suggestive fingertip from her wrist to her elbow.

She moved it out of his reach.

"Then I un-name you, Mercurio. Take yourself off and summon my handmaidens." Her tone sounded certain, but her dark eyes held increasing doubt. "Some adventure has come upon me in my rest, and I desire their remedy." She stood abruptly, stepping further yet away from him.

Mercurio rose too, but slowly, this time angling himself away from her and repressing a sigh. Even a trickster couldn't flimflam everyone. And he wasn't scoundrel enough to take her against her will.

For, yes, she was spurning him alright.

He sank down on the couch she'd vacated, scraped

his tunic up from the floor and draped it across his lap in full surrender.

"Okay. You won't play. I get that. But what *are* you doing here. And who are you? This is *my* bed chamber, you know."

Her eyes widened. "I'm Lixy, but . . ." She swallowed. "I'm not in Helicon, between the Agonippe and Hippocrene Springs, with Eupheme to attend me, am I?"

My, she was far from home. He'd never heard of those places.

And she was looking frightened. No, no, that would never do. Mercurio scrambled to climb back into his rumpled tunic. When his head emerged from the linen folds, she looked better. Amused?

He stood and bowed, flourishingly, ridiculously, and said, "I bid you welcome to my demesne, the second celestial sphere, the essence of the orbit of Mercury, and yours to order as you will, fair immortal. Command me!"

Her lips twitched. Containing laughter? Better and better.

He glanced around his chamber. Reasonably tidy, yes. Dark chestnut hangings covering the walls. Pedestals bearing various mechanical toys. (He did like geared things.) Glass-globed gas sconces, plus a scattering of small chests, footstools, and backless chairs. The ideal man cave.

But not, perhaps, the best spot for this interview. He should move this Lixy along before her amused and confused mixture – adorable as it looked on her – went stale again.

"Nectar, my lady? Ambrosia? Sol's cupbearer chose well this declension."

He gestured her to precede him through the archway. She'd be happier in the gallery on the other side of the portal hall.

"Oh! I am hungry! And thirsty."

She jumped up and almost scampered ahead of him. But the conservatory waylaid her, just as it had him. She passed through the arcade into its green tangle and deluge of light, holding up her arms so that the folds of her peplos fell away from her shoulders. Lovely shoulders.

"I was so cold," she explained. "So cold, and your demesne was so lovely warm."

"Memory returning? That's good." A little too hearty. He must watch his tone, if he wanted her comfortable. Nuance was everything. He wasn't sure exactly what he did want here, but tense and uneasy definitely wasn't it.

A little of the tightness around her eyes had

returned. "No . . . just the cold and . . . my limbs so weary. And your primary looked so inviting, fierce and golden. Your home so warm. Just that moment."

"The rest will come." There, that was better. Easy and confident without undue emphasis.

She grimaced and followed him back out of the conservatory.

When they passed through the portal hall, she glanced around, eagerly taking in its geared magnificence, but not pausing. Mercurio scooped up the tray with the nectar and noticed that three bowls of ambrosia fruits had been added to the array – in cream, cherry, and chocolate flavors by the scent of them. Excellent. He wouldn't have to plead at Hebe's shrine for extra servings.

The archway at the other end of the portal hall, intimate in scale, led directly into the gallery, a low-ceilinged balcony looking out onto the grand hall of clocks – water clocks. Nearly thirty of these contrivances filled the space, the largest a fountain-sized basin whose outflow turned the gears of an orrery, spinning vast Sol in its center, while far Pluto crept along the outer rim. Occupying a smaller footprint, but extending to the apex of the vault above, was his tower clock, shaped like a castle bastion with electrum crenellations at the top. Gears were involved there as well, moved by a hidden waterfall to turn hands on a broad clockface and spring a mechanical jester on the hour, clashing cymbals.

Mercurio watched Lixy's alert attention bloom into wonder again.

So she hadn't explored his home on the sly. She really had arrived dazed and faint, as she told it, and crawled onto the first soft surface that offered: his couch.

He ushered her to a pair of divans where the balcony bulged outward and the balustrade diminished to provide a better view. She didn't sit immediately, studying the spectacle before her. "These are clepsydrae, no?" She looked away from the hall to meet his gaze, her own friendly. "I'd heard of them."

Mercurio smiled at her. "They're a special interest of mine," he confessed. "Vigilem thinks it's silly, given that the passage of celestial time registers in my head more accurately than these mechanisms. Why bother?"

Lixy's brow quirked slightly. Puzzled?

"Vigilem's my cat," he explained. "Keeps watch whenever I'm otherwise occupied."

And how he wished he were otherwise occupied right now, exploring erotic delight with his visitor. But no, it was time he stopped hankering after impossibilities and devoted himself to delighting her more prosaically. Hard to do. She was just so luscious!

He poured her a goblet of nectar – still apricot – and used the electrum serving tongs to transfer an assortment of the ambrosia fruits to a saucer, then placed both drinking vessel and plate on the tripod table beside the nearer divan. He sank onto the farther seat, while she reclined on hers. Drawn by the food and drink at last.

"Mmm! What is this?" Her sip of the nectar was dainty. "We usually have apple at home. Sometimes pear. But Phrosyne loves apple, so we have apple. A lot. This good!"

"Apricot," he answered her.

"Thank you for your hospitality." Was she blushing again? "You must have wondered when you found me. Trespassing and claiming that you were."

Better slide over that. He didn't want to be thinking of secluded chambers with couches in them right now.

"But I understand perfectly. You had traveled far, too far, and exhaustion claimed you. I'm pleased my demesne stood near to provide you refuge. And happy for your company while you recover."

"Oh! I can stay for a time? It won't discommode you?"

"Perish the thought! I've lived alone with my cat

for too long. Perhaps Synchronia sent you my direction to shake me up a little." If so, boy did she succeed!

Lixy's smile wavered.

"But I'm not shaken. I'm glad. Perhaps you could contribute an idea or two to the gala celebration I'm planning. It's our primary's twenty-fifth anniversary, you see. I'm in charge of the spectacle for it, and I've encountered a slight hitch in my preparations."

Her smile returned, so he forged ahead, explaining his idea for a circus of the constellations. And she liked it, laughing with delight when he described the tumbling routine he envisioned for the Simiae, shading into awe at his word picture of the winged bulls and the ring of fire. But she was yawning again by the time the food ran out.

She *had* been hungry.

Vigilem materialized to surreptitiously lick the dregs from Mercurio's goblet, and then nudge Lixy's trailing hand for attention.

"Oh!" She lifted her head from the slanted rest of her divan and noodled the cat's ears.

Mercurio performed introductions. "Vigilem will look after you while I'm gone." And he did need to be going. Sol's birthday was approaching fast, and Mercurio had another eighteen constellations to visit, plus the boon to beg of Haden.

"Pleased to greet you, Vigilem. Thank you!" Lixy was polite to a fault, decided Mercurio. Perhaps she'd loosen up after she felt more at home.

"'Gilem! Didn't we used to have a guest suite somewhere? Next to Ceres' shrine? Or Fornax's."

"We did, metronome mover. It now houses your workbench and parts repository." Vigilem sounded smug. He often chided Mercurio about his hobby.

"I'll just curl up here," offered Lixy. Her eyelids drooped, not in the suggestive way that Mercurio enjoyed in a woman, but because sleep weighed them. And she might have to make do with this overly firm divan. But Mercurio didn't like it. *I want her to feel safe,* he realized. *And she can't after the stupid way I . . . she needs her own space. With a portal that closes. And a key she alone controls.*

Mercurio felt his shoulders sagging. Became aware of the funk of his unwashed tunic and his unwashed self. Despite his unexpected guest – delightful in so many ways – this had been a bad day.

C'mon Veloxus, think, think, think! You're the god of cunning and wit. Get a clue!

And then, suddenly, he knew.

It was tempting to simply tumble onto the couch in a heap and let sleep take her. That's what she'd done when she first arrived. With its alarming aftermath: waking under the lascivious gaze of a strange male.

No. She wouldn't make the same mistake twice.

So, here she was, properly removing her hair ribands and brushing her long tresses in appropriate seclusion. She definitely liked the seclusion, even if it was most . . . unexpected!

She placed the brush back down on the marble top of the dressing table and studied the space in the mirror.

The bronze bars forming the walls of the lift cage followed beautifully stylized patterns – art deco was what Mercurio'd said – but weren't conducive to either privacy or comfort. She'd drawn the hangings of aqueous gauze first of all – their bronze rings singing on the bronze rod – to create the impression that she resided within a diving jar beneath ocean waves. Then the heavier muffling draperies of turquoise velvet.

And then turned the massive key in the lock securing the strange collapsing mesh of the double doors that formed the front wall of the lift.

Ka-chunk.

After Mercurio bade her peaceful slumbers and turned on his heel. He'd scared her there at the beginning, but turned reasonable so quickly, she wasn't sure what to think. But she didn't want to be so rude as to lock her door in his face.

Why did he have both a lift and a grand stairway?

Silly question. With all those clocks, the feline automaton, and gears everywhere in his demesne, of course he had an elevator. At least it was generously proportioned. No, she'd not wake thinking herself in her own chambers on Mount Helicon. Which was all to the good. But it was at least the size of a handmaiden's closet, with room for couch and chest and dressing table with backless chair, and no likelihood of stumbling into the furnishings when walking around.

Amazing how rapidly Mercurio and Vigilem had turned a bare bronze cell into a lady's bower.

The cat dragged linens from a linen cupboard, while his master dragged the heavier appointments from a box room. When she emerged from the lavatory, it was ready for her. With fresh garments laid ready on the couch. (Did he regularly entertain lady friends? To have feminine clothing so immediately at hand?)

She turned back to herself in the mirror. No tangles remained in her curly mane. *Can I sleep now?* If Eupheme were with her, Lixy would be whining. Since she wasn't . . . Lixy divided the dark mass into three parts and began to braid them. Her arms felt leaden.

But her hair would be impossible later, if she didn't. And it didn't take long. She wrapped the end with a tasseled cord from the dressing table and pushed to her feet.

Should she activate the lift and descend into the hoistway?

Vigilem had explained how the mechanism worked. And the caged enclosure emerging through the floor of the lift foyer seemed an exposed location. But she was so tired. And Mercurio wasn't even home. He'd said he had a neighbor to visit. Plus the draperies were thick and opaque.

I'm going to sleep.

She pulled back the silken turquoise coverlet on the couch, then the cream sheeting, and slipped beneath them. A faint scent of lavender hung about the bed clothes. *Mmm.* And the pillows were soft.

If only she could tap that knowledge of herself that she could feel hovering at the edge of her awareness. She knew her name and that of her old nurse. But who was she really? In her core, her essence. And where was this second sphere, to which she'd come? And why had she been traveling anyway?

He'd lit the flambeaus once more, but not with fire.

Warmth – of sight and of touch – belonged to Proserpina. Haden would not profane her memory by gifting it to her absence.

Cold phosphor radiated from the wicks of the dark candles on their iron trees, brighter than the dim lumescence he called from rock and water, less friendly. The throne room seemed the frigid hell that mortals named it, blue-black pillars and walls, green-black vault above, and purple-black dais below.

"I open my court," he advised the petitioner before him. "And offer you a peerage within it."

She was not the first to whom he'd spoken those words, nor the tenth. Many a plutino had sought his presence since he'd unbarred the portals to the spheres beyond. But she possessed more savvy than her predecessors.

A tinge of annoyance crossed the ghastly ectoplasm of her face, softened by its veil. Delicate cheekbones, dainty nose, the remains of beauty, were she living rather than dead. Did her hand twitch beneath her draperies? The shadowy lace of her head covering, the fringes of her dark shawl, and the opalescence of her cloudy skirts obscured her almost entirely. Yet the thin, slight energy of her form manifested through her concealments.

"How shall I induce one of the great ones to do my bidding? What honors do you offer them through me? And how shall I maintain my dignity when they outweigh me here?"

No, not naïve at all.

"You may claim all that you may hold. Hold much, and they must honor you."

Another annoyed quirk twitched her countenance. "When a duchess moves, a mere lady must give way. My powers cannot claim and hold a duchy." She paused. "Unless you back me."

Haden sat, silent, but she did not crumble under the uncomfortable pause. Perhaps she might claim and hold a duchy. None of the others had thought to ask. None of the others withstood his gravity.

He reached for the tripod stand at his right hand, lifting a morsel of ambrosia to his lips. None of the fruits of Gaia, this. A creation of his own ninth sphere with the sour taste of fear, the bitterness of regret. Haden savored their burden on his tongue.

And swallowed.

"I have not many duchies to grant."

"You have granted none," she stated flatly.

How did she know?

"Grant one to me." So quiet, yet filled with authority.

"How if I offer a county?"

"A countess must yield precedence to her betters. I would yield it only to you."

Yes, this one might claim even a principality with her will. Could he suffer a princess in his midst? Or should he destroy her before she challenged him. The sweet stench of rot came faintly to his nostrils from her gown – her death clothing.

"My message to the great ones through you must be strong. *Will* they do your biding, if I raise you high? *Will* they tow the Teleio Mauro across my threshold?"

"Oh, yes." Softly still. "Even as I persuade you to my duchy, so will I bring them to ferry your ultimate darkness through the ninth sphere and inward."

Haden shivered, drawing his toga more closely about his torso. Draco was right. He did have the power to steal Chalcedonie's umbral quintessence.

"What will you forfeit should they refrain?" he asked.

She laughed. Awful crackling laughter. "Whatever you can claim and hold from me," she answered.

Almost she was worthy . . . of much more than a duchy. But he concluded their bargain with merely that. He would grant her great rank, and she would bend the great ones – the spirits of dark energy and the spirits of dark matter – to fetch his prize.

Haden smiled. And let her go.

Mercurio stood staring at the antechamber to Haden's throne room. Essentially a stark cube of emptiness carved from blackest basalt, the unadorned walls were washed by ultraviolet blue and green light, with a double colonnade at the far end.

Ugh! What a dark, dank hole of a place!

And why? Haden could have anything he wanted. Did he really want this?

Mercurio shook his head, thinking of his own home: warm and golden and alive with moving gears and clanking levers. He wished he were there now. There was a reason he avoided the ninth sphere. It even smelled . . . well, not musty or moldy, he admitted. He wanted it to smell moldy. It *should* smell of mold and mildew. But it didn't. Cold and clean like snowy mountains, despite its underground milieu. Huh. He preferred the cinnamon of home.

He dragged his attention back to the dim bronze mirror inset on one of the blank side walls. His long formal tunica in his favorite amber was largely hidden by the careful folds of his longest, most aristocratic toga in dazzling white. Flawless for high diplomacy.

Not that it mattered. None of the colors showed true in this odd lighting.

It would be his words, not his garb, that prevailed here. Or not.

A court functionary, robed in black and wearing the eyeless mask dictated by the ninth sphere's master, beckoned Mercurio forward. At least Haden had summoned his servants back when he opened his court. All the rumors said he'd been sulking alone in the shadows for the last quarter of Sol's galactic year. Disturbing his solitude . . . Mercurio wouldn't have done it.

Mercurio nodded to the functionary and passed through the double row of columns dividing the anteroom from Haden's throne hall. His sandals, wings furled, slapped dully against the polished stone floor. Strange reflections ran away from him on the shiny surface as he moved.

On the other side of the arcade, no courtiers clustered in the wide, rectangular crypt – larger than the anteroom, but just as plain. Haden's court might be open, but it was not populated. Not yet.

Of course, Mercurio welcomed no retinue either. Before Lixy had arrived, his warm and inviting abode held him alone. Him and his cat, Vigilem. Maybe it wasn't fair to accuse his uncle of being a nasty old recluse.

Mercurio gritted his teeth together. Cronos, no! It was fair. *He's an old hermit. And I'm not!*

Phosphorescent flambeaus, placed at intervals along the blank walls and clustered behind the paired thrones – if you could call two blocks of granite thrones, painted the space with cones of acid green and purple radiance.

Haden sat unmoving on his royal bench. Backlit, he seemed more shadow and silhouette than living figure.

"Mercurio Veloxus Ludificor." Haden intoned Mercurio's full name without welcome. "It is long since you last entered my presence."

Yes, well, there's a reason for that, thought Mercurio, still approaching. Did Haden think to dismay him so easily?

"You could always visit me," he suggested. Hah! Just the right amount of insouciance in that remark. *I've got you nailed, uncle mine. It's my lucky day, and my tongue's flapping at both ends.* "Do you good! A little sunlight, a little warmth. Get a tan!"

"What boon do you bring before me that I may grant it? I seriously doubt you visit merely to invite me to your overly hot demesne."

Mercurio fetched up at the double steps to the dais, took them in one stride.

"Would you accept? If I did invite you?" He stepped deliberately closer, too close, to make Haden look up.

Haden looked down, apparently examining the signet ring on his left hand. "You will have to issue the invitation and await my response. Youngling."

Mercurio bounced on his toes and noticed the tripod tray at Haden's knee. The usual nectar and ambrosia, but it smelled like nothing reasonable to consume. Musky and strange. He resisted the urge to snabble a dainty, unasked, even though doing so would annoy Hades most beautifully.

"I wanted to consult. About Sol's birthday."

"Ah, yes. Your purview this galactic year. First time, isn't it?" Haden ceased studying his ring, gazing through the columns across from his bench. "Better you than me." He sniffed, then raised his voice. "Ianitos! You may retire!"

The functionary, lingering in the anteroom, bowed and departed.

Haden's attention came back to Mercurio. "So. You need help, do you?"

"Perhaps. Are you inclined to give it?"

"Unlikely."

"I thought not. But . . ." Mercurio trailed deliberately into nothing, then drawled, "I might help you."

Silence. Then a slight motion from Haden's shrouded figure. Was that amusement that Mercurio detected?

"And how would youthful naivete serve my need?" Yes, Haden was entertained. By something. Best to be a bit coy.

"Are all your desires perfect? Fulfilled and unyearning?"

"I extinguished them long ago." Haden shifted, then stood, abruptly tall, respecting Mercurio's space no more than Mercurio had respected his. "State your business. Dancing like a moth about the candle flame does no more than prolong your certain end. And I weary."

No, Mercurio refused to let Haden dictate the course of the conversation. They were fighting. With words, yes, but the words of immortals carried weight, carried repercussion, carried . . . much.

I must unsheathe my sword.

"I chatted with Proserpina on my way home from the last conclave. She quite likes the fourth sphere. Green and bowery, you know." Mercurio's lips stretched in a not-nice smile, and he didn't step back from Haden's intimidating height.

"Get out." Haden's command emerged utterly flat.

Mercurio slouched one foot forward, placed his right fist on his right flank to cock the elbow outward. "No."

"I could compel you."

"No doubt. But nonetheless, my business is Proserpina."

"Your business is never Proserpina."

"The next time Hebe grants you a pomegranate, you will count the seasons more that you wish her to linger by your side, and save that number of pips. Preserve them within the cage of a dead woman's mouth for a night. Bathe them in the waters of the Styx for another."

"How dare you recount my sins to me as though freshly born and presented for my delectation anew!" Haden's hand clamped onto Mercurio's forearm, cold like stone, adamant like stone, bruising in its strength. Mercurio felt warmth leaving his body, exiting through Haden's grasp. "Never. Mention. Her. Again."

Mercurio's throat grew chill, his lips, his tongue. "I would offer her them at my table, and she would swallow them unsuspecting," he choked out.

Haden let go so suddenly, Mercurio staggered. Warmth came flooding back into him, the relief of it inexpressible.

Haden unwrapped his toga from his head and upper body, tossing it on his bench. The black light of the flambeaus picked out his neat, curling beard, his chiseled nose, his broad brow. The silk of his tunica, long like Mercurio's own, glimmered faintly, metallic, but without hue. Was it woven of silver thread? Gold?

"So . . . you do possess coin." Haden turned half away from Mercurio, his profile caught by light, his eyes at last revealed. Bereft? "What would you buy with it?"

Ah! Now! Now, was his moment. Mercurio spoke. "The great ones of the void traverse your far reaches, kiss the edges of the ninth sphere, whisper along the outer winds at Sol's vast heliopause. Should you speak, they will listen. Should you, their neighbor, request, they might grant it."

This time Haden's amusement pushed a dry snicker from his lips. "And having my coin, not theirs, you ask me to ask them." He shook his head. "Very well. What would you have me ask them?"

Now they were talking. Mercurio explained his dilemma. "I need some way to ensure the elder cousins participate in Sol's celebration. I think they

want to. And I have this fabulous spectacle planned. But imagine if Ganymede and Juventa blow the trumpets and my first act fails to appear. It won't do!"

Haden pinned his upper lip with a lower tooth. "And you believe the great ones – Umbra and Semotus – wield power enough to compel the constellations?"

"Not directly, no. But there is a force, once summoned, that no one – mortal or immortal – can resist. On the tide of the Teleio Mauro, the elder cousins will come to shore. Once there . . ."

". . . your silver tongue will do the rest, should they continue reluctant."

Mercurio grinned. "Yes."

"Let us discuss this bargain of yours."

Cronos, but bed felt good! The lighting, dim and soothing. His chamber, surrounding him with its friendly brown tones, inviting. His couch, cushiony firm and silken. Ah!

Mercurio pulled a second pillow toward his shoulder and under his head, pushed the top sheet down to his waist.

It was too warm for any heavy coverlet, too warm for more than half the sheet, even though he'd arrived chilled and shivering. But triumphant. With three pips of a pomegranate now held safe in a cedar box on his altar in Haden's shrine.

The journey back from the ninth sphere had been grueling.

It always was. Pluto swung so far into the void, far and farther from Sol's warmth. The trip inward took days, even translating from sphere to sphere, the way the planetaries did it, rather than flying as the elder cousins and other celestial beings must travel. And the outer spheres were so devouring cold! Icy ninth, chill eighth, misting seventh.

Grimy droplets of Saturnian rain mixed with the melting ice of Plutonian rime on Mercurio's skin and garments by the time he'd stood in his home portal hall at last. Almost he'd sunk to the textured floor, a sodden and exhausted heap, asleep on the spot. But the aroma of steamed chocolate mixed with banana revived him. Hebe's choice was perfect again.

The heat of the chocolate nectar stilled his shivers, and the banana custard ambrosia sent a trickle of energy to his leaden limbs.

He dragged himself past his bed chamber just far enough to peek into the lift foyer and check on his guest. The lift that was her bower reposed quiescently within the hoistway forming a massive mesh column in the center of the domed space. The turquoise curtains were drawn, unruffled by any movement within. No sounds emerged. Was Lixy still sleeping? Or . . . more likely, sleeping again?

He saw Vigilem's tail disappearing down the curving stair that sank out of sight along the foyer's outer wall. *I'll ask him later.* Bed! Bed was calling.

He'd skipped bathing. Falling asleep in the bath – not a possibility, but a certainty – and half drowning before he awoke held no appeal. Dropping his soaked toga and tunica (no loin cloth present in formal regalia) on the lavatory's tiles and toweling off would have to suffice.

Even now, eyes half shut as he drifted toward sleep, he could smell the dried salt of exertion on his body, overlaid by the rock of the ninth sphere and the brine from the outer triad of the seventh – Neptunus Equester's demesne.

But he'd succeeded! He'd done it! Persuaded Haden to summon the force that would ensure the spectacle in Sol's honor was worthy. Yes!

"I'll bathe when I awake," he murmured. And then sleep swept him under.

He knew he was dreaming, and it did no good.

The mansion – or this wing of it; it was hard to tell the full extent of the place – was a long, tall, narrow structure. On its second floor, a spare corridor ran down its center, flanked by modest rooms to each side.

It was night, and he stood in that corridor, young and scared, his head perhaps hip high to an adult, had any been present to protect him.

The doors, so many closed doors, were all French ones. Some showed the white roller shades pulled down behind their panes – part way, or all the way to the threshold. Many were unshaded, their glass dark on his right, and passing through a flood of moonlight on his left. The moon had risen on that side of the house. Gazing through the door window nearest him, he could see her generous disk sailing the midnight sky beyond the triple-sashed window in the room.

Oh, Cronos, if only he were there, safe on the moon's white breast or sleeping on her silver couch.

Instead, he was here, frozen in terror, feeling horror at his back, somewhere beyond the open door between this corridor and the stair hall five doors behind him. Distant, but coming.

Coming for him.

He strained his ears. Nothing. Nothing.

He looked again at the polished wooden floor boards beside his bare toes and the terrible residue on them. Like ink, but not ink.

It painted the portrait of a boy like him: young enough to need his nurse, fear-drenched eyes, and mouth open in a scream.

But it wasn't him, wasn't Mercurio.

The boy wore strange clothes: a fitted white tunic with long tight sleeves and a great wide collar; a snug loin garment with attached leg coverings to the knees; and smooth hose on his calves.

That boy was dead.

Mercurio shuddered. And heard a stirring behind him, the hush of terror brushing the floor, less heard than sensed. Not on the floor boards of the stair hall, no. Perhaps on the stairs?

Oh, Gaia, help! If only she could. If only she knew.

He fought the numbness gripping his limbs, reached out a trembling hand to the door knob. Its metal – bronze, he guessed – felt cool to his touch.

He turned it, cringing at the scritching springy sound that resulted.

He tasted sour bile in the back of his throat and swallowed, hard.

The door eased open, its hinges blessedly silent. Thank you! The faint scent of beeswax breathed from the room into the corridor.

Another exhalation sounded behind him, a sighing, low and long.

Oh, Cronos!

He moved his unshod left foot. No winged sandals in his youth.

The floor board squeaked as his weight left it.

Came another movement of air in the stairwell.

Thin carpet covered the floor within the side chamber, patterned and worn. Its wool threads felt good on the sole of his foot. The floor boards beneath it did not creak as he stepped on them.

He lifted his right foot.

All remained quiet, and he passed over the threshold.

A tall, dark grandfather clock – not ticking – loomed against one wall, with an equally tall secretary desk opposite it. Two spindle-backed chairs in front of the window cast dark stripes across the carpeting.

Mercurio shut the French door behind him, wincing at the loud click of the closing latch tab.

He stretched up and up on tiptoes.

Could he reach the hanging pull string of the roller shade?

Just barely, his fingertips bumped the dangling, crocheted ring. Its slight weight moved away. Then he had it, firmly gripped between thumb and forefinger, and pulled it down, all the way down, past the lowest panes of the door's window, pull string huddled in a tangle on the carpet.

Oh, Gaia! If only there were no crack under the door, connecting the air of his sanctuary – this room – to that of the corridor.

Something out there shifted. No sound this time, just a sense of presence, growing and growing and . . . now!

It was here on the second floor.

Eyes starting in his face, Mercurio crept out of the moonlight throwing his shadow across the carpet and onto the door shade.

Had it seen him? Did it know he was here? Right here?

Another shifting, a louring immanence, and then a hushing sound he could hear. No mere hint or suggestion of sound.

This was real.

It was coming.

Mama! He stifled a whimper.

It was sliding along the floor of the corridor.

Closer.

And closer.

Were he out there awaiting it . . . his fate would be the fate of the boy ironed onto the floor, his essence vacuumed by the devourer, his residue left to paint the wood with his terrified portrait.

He awoke gasping, sitting abruptly, and drenched in sweat.

Lixy stood just inside the doorway of the darkened bed chamber, uncertain how to proceed.

The bright gas lights in the corridor behind her brought a sharp arch of carpeting into vibrant clarity – warm brown wool woven with traceries of amber, russet, and copper – but little else. Her eyes strained to discern the couch and its sleeper.

Not possible.

I just wanted to get out the last time I was here. Why am I back?

The incoherent shout that drew her had not been repeated, but she could hear the gasping pants of someone striving to bring his breathing under control.

"Mercurio?"

No answer, but the wild breathing abruptly quieted.

"Shall I bring you refreshment? The nectar's citrus this morning, and the ambrosia's coconut."

A croak, then throat clearing.

"I'm okay."

More throat clearing and a grunt. Then some rustling, and she heard his footfalls approaching across the carpet.

A much rumpled Mercurio emerged from the shadows. He'd draped his bedsheet around him as a makeshift toga.

"Did I wake you?" he asked, looking sleepy and stressed at the same time, hazel eyes blinking against the bright corridor lights, but with lingering horror in them, curly chestnut hair, tousled.

"Sorry about that. Bad dream," he explained.

Yes, she'd guessed. "I was just breaking my fast, when I heard you yell."

Lixy smiled at him, hoping to diffuse any male embarrassment.

"Oh." A tide of red flushed his face. "Gotcha." He scrubbed a hand across his eyes and cheekbones.

Well, that had worked poorly.

"I didn't think 'Gilem would suffocate you in

your sleep, but who knows?" She winked.

He laughed. "That used to happen when I first set him going. Even though he's not a born creature, he behaved like a kitten. And thought I was his mother. My face was his favorite sleeping spot."

Oh, much better.

"I have a companion animal at home who does that."

Except . . . where exactly was home? She still didn't know. In spite of some serious navigational conversations with Vigilem while Mercurio was away, along with a marathon of praying at the two dozen shrines in his demesne. She'd thought that might help, but it hadn't.

In spite of the strange reverse familiarity of her devotions.

She could feel her petition go out from her and through each shrine's presiding deity. But then it dissipated, when it should concentrate. And nothing caught it. Someone should catch it. *She* should catch it. She shook her head. It made no sense.

"Has 'Gilem taken care of you while I was away?" pursued Mercurio. "I didn't mean to be gone quite so long."

She subdued her slight start. "Oh, yes. Thank you. I've been very comfortable."

Or she would have been, were it not for her continuing confusion. She'd spent a lot of her time sunbathing in the conservatory, craving the heat and extreme radiance as though starved for them. That had been delicious. As had the unfamiliar flavors served by this system's cupbearer. But she hated not knowing who she was and where she belonged and what she was doing. Or supposed to be doing.

"Sure you don't want me to bring you anything? Ambrosia helps me chase away a nightmare."

The corner of his mouth twitched up. Clearly Mercurio was recovering his poise.

"Oh, I'll dine," he assured her. "After I bathe!" He wrinkled his nose, then grinned. "I wouldn't stand too close, were I you, milady."

She was already close enough to smell him. Dried old sweat, new fear sweat, and under it all a pleasing masculine savor. Closing her eyes and inhaling would be . . . embarrassing. She grinned back at him instead.

"I'll leave you to it then."

He bowed and retreated.

She returned to her interrupted repast.

The jungle of the Simiae lay far around the arc of the eighth sphere from Draco's cave.

Perched on the topmost twigs of the massive black trees or curled among their roots, you enjoyed the same panorama of the vast starfield, jeweled lights flung across velvety night.

But Mercurio sat on one of the middle branches, a mammoth limb nearly as broad as his elevator's floor back home, and the spreading lavender-gray leaves above and below hid the view. He could feel rough bark pressing into his thigh.

It had seemed rude to hover midair on his sandals when old Jyutping, the patriarch of the tribe, hunkered below.

Mercurio studied the wild wrinkled face opposite his. Dark, dark skin, almost purple. Deep sad eyes with a gleam of unexpected humor at their nadir. Surrounded by a blue mane, ashen at its hair tips.

Jyutping gave him back look for look. "You bear a dark cloak on your shoulders, young one," he said, raising a skeptical, furry brow.

Mercurio glanced right and down, glanced left.

Just the bronze shoulder brooches holding his tunic up. No cloak.

The constellations, for all their ancient pageantry and honor, weren't stuffy like Haden was. No need to trip over the long tunica or to strangle in the voluminous folds of his toga to please them. This short garb, paired with a loin brief for modesty, required much less managing. He preferred it for travel, despite the cool ambience of the outer spheres.

"I don't see anything," he said.

"No, you wouldn't." Jyutping's lips quirked up. He stretched his long ape arms toward a narrow branch above himself and bounced on his hind limbs. Next moment he was swinging to and fro.

Mercurio's gaze followed him: back and forth, then twirling up in a somersault around the upper bough, and abruptly down again, squatting beside Mercurio.

"Papaya?" Jyutping handed him the fruit of a tender-skinned ambrosial variety and grinned. "The shadow's not in your essence, Veloxus, but pinned to your soul."

That sounded alarming, but Mercurio had other priorities right now. Best to close the deal before Jyutping developed second thoughts. The floral scent of papaya rose from the fruit in his palm, tempting him. He ignored it.

"So you'll do it? Just when Mercury finishes transiting Sol, you and your troupe will arrive and begin."

The loud swoosh of a hurtling Simius smacked through the leaves at Mercurio's elbow.

He lurched, startled, but wasn't fast enough to see the passerby. The two chasing after made him blink. Even in the gloom of this dusky jungle, the brilliant vermilion pelt of the one and the vivid viridian of the other stood out.

"Hold out for creative license!" yelled the viridian Simius.

"Mercurio's not a dud like Haden," shouted the vermillion one. "He knows how to have fun! Salve, Mercurio! Quomodo es?" *How are you?*

Then they were gone, although Mercurio could hear their passage, down and down, then swooping up and away.

Jyutping leapt after them, disappearing in their wake for a moment, then breaking off his rattling chase to reappear over the far curve of the floor branch. He settled at Mercurio's other side.

"We'll design the performance and arrive at transit's end. Done!" He reached out his arm, grasped Mercurio's right bicep, waited for Mercurio to grip his, and shook their arms once, emphatically: the Simian vow of agreement.

"I'm looking forward to seeing it," Mercurio told him.

"You should be." Jyutping bared his teeth. "It'll be like nothing the Simiae have done before." The humor lurking in his old eyes woke to renewed life. "Be ready!" And he was gone again, on the trail of his active nephews.

Mercurio nibbled his lip. Strange how cooperative everyone had been following his bargain with Haden. Could they sense he was more than a beggar? That he had power in the transaction that he'd lacked before?

Maybe.

But he felt just the same to himself. Except a little dizzy right now. The physical agility and comedy of the Simiae, when juxtaposed against their sage judgment, bewildered him. Absentmindedly, he bit into the papaya. Its juicy sweetness filled his mouth and dripped down his chin. *Mmm.*

What would Lixy make of the Simiae?

He found himself wishing he'd invited her along. Or that he was returning home to dine with her before making his next pitch. Her company satisfied a loneliness he'd not known he had.

I wonder if she might stay for a good long visit – say a galactic year – if I invited her.

He liked that idea. Vigilem's sarcastic remarks and solitary ways wouldn't seem quite enough after

Lixy departed. Maybe she could stay for longer. Two years. Or five.

"Cave infra!" *Watch out below!* A turquoise Simius swooped above Mercurio's helmeted head, plucked the half-eaten papaya from his fingers, and soared away with a cackle. "Sanum esse, consobrinum!" *Be well, cousin.*

Mercurio shook his head. Time to get moving. The cliffs of the winged bulls were a long way around the circle of the eighth sphere from here.

He leapt into the ether, sandal wings flapping.

"I feel nothing," stated Haden.

The throne room of his demesne glowed more brightly than before, the shadows fewer and less dense, the phosphor concentrated. He'd ordered the greens magnified, and they flooded the rock walls and the shallow curve of the upper vault. The purple punctuations of the flambeaus could not spread beyond their iron trees.

Ianitos attended him, still in shrouding robes and eyeless face mask, but close by Haden's bench, not at a distance in the antechamber.

"My king, a great one approaches," Ianitos murmured, bowing. The brocade of his garment rustled stiffly. "What is your will?"

"Know you who advances to my court? Milord? Or milady?" Haden stroked his beard, neatly combed, and touched the elaborate folds of his toga, purple for this occasion, though it looked black in the green illumination. The upper length of the wool swathed his shoulders, removed from his head. Cool against his brow, the iron diadem, visible now, signified his sovereignty.

"Milord Semotus, my king."

Still Haden felt nothing. Neither the weight of dark power, nor the indrawing of deepest shadow.

"Bid him approach my presence and be welcome."

Ianitos moved swiftly away, descending from the dais and gliding across the vast black floor – the one truly lightless element in the phosphorescent space. He passed into the colonnade and out through the antechamber.

Haden lifted the goblet resting on the tripod tray at his elbow and sipped. Chilled cucumber nectar spiked with mint soothed his throat. He noticed his back straightening, the crown of his head rising, the base of his spine rooting downward.

He felt . . . not happy, no, but interested. Outward focused for the first time in . . . too long.

Something coalesced in the promenade beyond the antechamber – hidden from sight by the closed iron portal and its stone architrave – but palpable to some other sense, louring, a tidal current drawing inward to an unfathomable locus.

Then Haden did see his guest, despite the stone and metal barriers.

Semotus' cloaking hood loomed far overhead, penetrating some arcane dimension apart from water and rock and stardust, standing tall through the vaults of Haden's demesne, his shoulders blocking the northernmost constellations of the ecliptic. His robes swept down even further, through the lightless floor, to root within unguessed substance at the base of the cosmos. His face lay concealed behind an eyeless mask, like Ianitos', but far more terrible in aspect, matte black and radiating subtle death.

He was here, without moving, inhabiting Haden's throne room – a pontifex, an emperor, a god. Truly, the first duchess of Haden's new court, Milady Velato, Her Grace of Sedna, saw farther than had Pluto's guardian.

How shall I anchor my dominion when Semotus outweighs me a thousand fold?

"Why should I desire the ordering of a planetary orbit, when all the void between the stars is mine?" Semotus' voice sounded cold, so cold, and deep.

Haden had not realized he spoke his question aloud, that the great one should answer it. But he knew truth when he heard it. "I await your mercy, Majesty."

"My forbearance multiplies unnecessarily, Counselor. Where lie your roots?" Did the horror burning from Semotus' death mask grow less stern?

Haden exhaled, following his breath down and out, feeling the ties binding him to his planet and its great dance, feeling the suffusion of his essence within Pluto's ice and rock.

I am Pluto. Pluto is mine own, my heart.

"Push against me," Semotus ordered.

What foolishness. But Haden pushed, thrusting from his roots, from his heart.

And Semotus moved, shifted back to the throne room's antechamber.

"You see?" The great one's voice carried amusement beneath its chill tone, a strange undercurrent of faint warmth.

"I see." Relief settled in Haden's breast, passing outward through his being. All was well, then. "What wish you, that you pause here?"

"To tell you that I found the Teleio Mauro rolling

loose and nudged it. The essence of the dark has started its immense journey."

"You know this?"

"Counselor, while my left hand touches your sphere, the ninth of Sol" – he stirred his shrouded arm, quiescent at his side – "my right fetches absolute gravity to do your bidding. Did not your messenger utter this, your desire?"

"Ah," Haden breathed. "Yes." And sipped once more from his goblet. The liquid sparkled warm and sharp on his tongue, cucumber no more, sweet raisin wine in its place. "And your gift, from my hand to yours? Your left?" Haden allowed a hint of warmth into his own voice.

"The Duchy of Orcus suffices."

"Then it is yours."

Lolloping down the last few steps into the foundations of his habitation, Mercurio found Lixy bending over the lefthand bank of instrumentation there.

The corridor leading away from the flight of stairs curved up slightly, its farther reaches disappearing from view in the downward curve of the ceiling. Smooth and slanting control surfaces – bronze, of course – ran along the bronze walls at waist height. Above them, on each side, a ribbon of window (or what looked to be window, really intricate displays connecting the physical reality to this essential one) gave marvelous views of his planet from a hundred Gaian miles up.

Mercury sighed satisfaction. What an incredible heavenly body. And his, all his.

Its dark gray crust – magnificently marked with vast craters, long sharp ridges, steep peaks, rumpled hills, and smooth stone seas – stretched from the horizon, seen through one long "window," under this "bridge," and on to the horizon visible through the "window" on the other side. Black sky topped it all, with Sol blaring intensely in the dark span.

Glorious!

The gauges and recording drum of his portal hall served for cursory checks while Mercurio came and went in his travels for his fellow planetaries.

But *this* was where the real work of tending Mercury was done.

Lixy turned her head and smiled. "What does this one measure?" She pointed to the dial she'd been staring at when he arrived.

Mercurio stepped from the lowest step to the textured bronze floor. Its diamond grips, larger and bumpier than upstairs, were rough under his bare feet. He strode to Lixy's side.

Cronos, it felt good to be here! With all the traveling for Sol's celebration, plus the usual messages between immortals, he'd scarcely been down these stairs since perihelion. Even the air was special here: with a hot smell like baked clay and a dry burnt taste on his tongue.

Mercurio bent his gaze to Lixy's dial. Ah, yes, that one. "It's the hot spot monitor," he said happily.

She crinkled her brow. "Volcanism? Your planet doesn't look geologically active."

Mercurio laughed. "Oh, its core's still alive. Molten and generating magnetism just as it should. In fact, the most iron-rich core in the system." He couldn't help boasting. His sphere was unique! "But you're right. The years of lava pouring from cracks in the crust or through impact holes made by meteors are long gone."

"Then how are there hot spots?" Lixy straightened and stretched.

Mercurio, distracted by the lovely rise of her bosom under her tunica, hurriedly returned his eyes to his lovely-in-a-different-way gauges and slide controls. He didn't want a repeat of their awkward first meeting. Lixy was relaxed around him now, and he wished her to stay so.

She's my guest. And I like her.

"Mercury rotates on its axis only three times for every two times it revolves around Sol," he explained.

"So it has a long day," Lixy judged.

"A very long day. Plus . . ."

Lixy tilted her head, curious for his further revelation.

". . . its orbit is very eccentric. At aphelion, it's forty-three million Gaian miles from Sol. While at perihelion, it's only twenty-nine million miles away."

"So when it's really close to your primary, the sun side bakes?" guessed Lixy.

"Exactly!"

Mercurio was pleased. Not only was she a quick pupil, but she was interested. None of his neighbors cared to learn the marvels of his planet. It wasn't really fair, because Mercury *was* marvelous. It deserved an appreciative audience. *At least there's me. And, now, there's Lixy.*

"Also . . ." Would she be willing to hear more?

"There's more?" Her eyes widened, but eagerly, not in dismay.

"At perihelion, Mercury moves much faster around Sol. Like a slingshot. So fast that it overtakes the speed of its rotation!" he explained. "Which means that the sun shines straight down on the same exact spot for several Gaian weeks. Which means that spot gets super hot!"

"Oh, cool!"

And she really did think it was cool. Mercurio could tell. And could really tell when she asked him another question. Had he discovered a sister aficionado of Sol's inmost planet? Maybe.

He was glad she'd taken him at his word to make free of his entire demesne. As busy as he'd been, he wasn't entertaining her properly. The least he could do was provide her with full access to his sphere so she could amuse herself.

He was also glad to find her somewhere other than the conservatory. She was welcome to stay wherever she wanted for as long as she wanted, but she seemed to get weak and muzzy when she didn't get enough sun. That worried him. He'd assumed her long journey had caused the extreme debilitation she experienced on her arrival. But why this continuing craving for Sol's rays?

"Can we come back here after the nuncheon?" she asked him as they climbed to learn what Hebe had given them. "I'm afraid your instruments tell me little, and I'd really like to learn more."

"Of course!" He needed to go petition the Pleiades, but for *this* – he'd make time.

Nuncheon was a delicate plum nectar and two ambrosias: lemon custard and chilled white grapes. They took it in the clock hall as usual and lingered over their meal. Lixy was just asking him about calibrating the clepsydra possessing the largest basin when she stopped mid-sentence with a startled look on her face.

"What is it?"

She didn't answer, her eyes faraway, as though she saw all the way to the center of the galaxy.

"Lixy?"

She began returning to the present place and time, to him, then drew a sharp breath through her nostrils, and looked into the distance again, sitting very still.

Mercurio surged to her side, reached out a hand to touch her shoulder, drew back in frustration, and shouted, "'Gilem! I need you!"

The cat ran through the arch from the portal hall, hissing. "Do not handle her, water notary!"

"I know that! But something's wrong. How do we help her?"

Lixy sighed and her eyes focused on his anxious face. "I am well."

"What happened? Are you sure?" Now he did touch her, clasping her hands – they were warm – and feeling her brow – not too warm.

She seemed well.

"I don't know what happened. Something within my essence . . . moved. That had been long still. I don't understand it."

"But you're normal now? It's gone back where it belongs?"

"No." Her tone was distant. "It moves yet."

Oh, Cronos! He didn't like the sound of that.

"Let's get you to the conservatory," he urged.

Lixy laughed. "I'm not ill."

But Vigilem added his persuasions to Mercurio's, and she appeased their wishes. Not unwillingly. The sunlight always called her.

Draco had flown far, far out, so far from his primary that Sol shone as one small point of light amidst countless others.

And, yet, as long as his wings clapped the solar wind of the heliosphere, his open maw tasted the peppery heat of Sol's photons, and his snout smelled their dry papery fragrance, he was home, wrapped in the soft night of Sol's cloak.

He'd buzzed icy Pluto, just to annoy Haden, and detoured to view oblong Haumea for her unusual shape. Buried Orcus and cold-burning Ixion were too distant to attract him on this trip.

For he flew to meet his destiny.

The Teleio Mauro was moving, and he would encounter it somewhere in the void between Sol and his nearest neighbor, Proxima Centauri.

The shock wave at the heliopause, where the solar wind escaped the magnetic grip of Sol's celestial spheres – all nine of them – tumbled him willy nilly. But plutinos grew scarce in the region. Not much for him to crash into. Rolling with the tumble, he recovered and avoided straining a wing as he had last time, a galactic year ago.

Beyond the heliopause, the void thinned. Colder, flatter, and scentless, it lacked the richness of home. Draco shivered and flew on.

And on.

And on.

The interval between the heliopause and the inward edge of the torus that formed the inner Oort Cloud was a long stretch, but all intervals grew long, so far from Sol's reach.

Eighty-three Gaian days later, he entered the Hill Cloud – the inner Oort – although he'd been seeing it for most of his journey.

First a soft haze clouding the spangle of stars at the center of the Milky Way, then strengthening to become a mist. As he drew closer, it went from mist to blanket of dust to a cloud of scintillating sparkles. And then he passed one, a spinning ball of ice flying under his wing, and another.

They clustered ever more thickly.

These were the comets, or the comets-to-be, awaiting the gravitational nudge that would send them hurtling toward Sol, soaring in a splendor of out-flashing tail. He could see their guardians, each kneeling on her diamond cushion, angel wings folded as she prayed.

The Hill Cloud spread even farther than had the long haul between the heliopause and its inner edge.

Draco tried engaging the guardian spirits, greeting them, posing questions, and offering conversation, but they ignored him, preferring their silent meditations.

He grew lonely.

A creature of the cosmos, he knew solitude, embraced it. But Sol's heliosphere was a crowded busy place compared to this. Even when the Great

Bear stayed home nurturing her little one, or Bootes remained busy herding his flock, Leo or Pegasus came calling. And Mercurio popped in and out with messages in a manner downright unrestful.

Draco knew days and weeks of solitude, sometimes months.

Traversing the inner Oort took two years; the outer Oort, another four.

The void was worse.

Who could have guessed that the company of silent immortals who ignored you – the comets – counted for company nonetheless?

The vast dark beyond the Oort went on forever.

Once a stray asteroid slammed by him. Nothing and nobody else.

Only when they were gone did he discover that the thin nothingness outside the heliopause had a taste – faint silver – and a smell like moonlight. The void beyond the Oort taught him true emptiness.

His wings wearied at last, and he grew hungry. Famished enough that he could taste the memory of his last coronal flare, savory and piquant and filling.

He'd never flown so far.

He changed his steady wing beat to a soaring motion, conserving his reserves, and flew onward.

Another Gaian year and another.

He hardly knew when the void acquired density, so gradual was the shift. From the thinnest of thinness, it became merely a thinnish thinness, and then not thin at all. Thick and rumpled, bumping him up and down, this way and that.

Was this Proxima Centauri's heliopause? Surely it was too soon. He'd have to fly another twenty Gaian years to get that far. And miss Sol's birthday, which would never do.

What was this?

The turbulence grew rougher, stronger. Tired as he was, he switched back to his more powerful wing stroke, thrusting into the flowing dark. It fought him, and he fought back.

And then he knew.

This was the Teleio Mauro! The vast, dark shockwave of the coming shadow, surging through the abyss between the stars, bearing down on the Proxume Sphaera, the "local bubble" in which Sol swung. Not here yet, but coming indeed.

Overwhelming pressure at last turned Draco aside.

He gave way before it, surrendering. Curling around to the right and sweeping on in a grand reversal, he split for home. Grateful, astonished, and wondering how he'd found what he was looking for

in this great sea of nothingness, but sure he'd received something he'd wanted, even though he didn't know what it was.

A desire for home?

If that were it, he possessed it munificently, his dragon heart crying out for . . . Sol.

Riding the great wave for home, he sang, deeply, powerfully, a resounding music of the wayward returned to the hearth.

Mercurio climbed to the top of the amphitheater's seating, leaping from one massive stone block up to the next, not bothering with a detour to the shallow risers near the edges of the curving tiers.

This was quicker, and the push and pull of his leg muscles felt good. He'd been standing still for too long, instructing his satyr helpers to, "Move it left a trifle, no a bit more, no that's too far," and so on.

He turned and surveyed the scene.

The white stones of the banked seating, the level semi-circular performance arena, and the vertical proscenium backdrop were clean and swept, ready for the festivities. And the two maypoles, each almost as tall as a sailing ship's mast and rising from trapdoors, stood straight.

Finally!

"Tighten the bolts!" he called down to the workers. "That's good!"

A flurry of activity began among the clustered satyrs, several bracing each pole while others wielded wrenches.

Mercurio allowed his attention to wander.

The day shone glorious, clear and warm with the lightest of breezes. The gentle folds of old, old mountains rolled away from the amphitheater, cloaked in forest and alive with fluting birds, dancing nymphs, and chasing fauns. The resinous scent of conifers floated in the soft air, along with distant laughter.

No wonder Proserpina preferred the fourth sphere, Gaia's, to the ninth, Haden's.

Mercurio hunched slightly in guilt.

She'd be getting much less of her summer holiday after this was over, chained to Pluto for an extra three months of the Gaian year. Still, she was *married* to Haden. It wasn't fair that she spent so much time away from her husband. Besides, she'd spent a lot longer than her allotted nine months this time. Well over three galactic years! What was up with that anyway?

Why hadn't Haden complained? Sol would have done something, if he'd said.

Mercurio shook his head. *Not my problem.*

The dusty smell of sun warmed limestone coaxed him away from worry toward ease.

The satyrs had finished their bolting task and were working the massive cranks behind the proscenium, their flailing arms flashing in and out of view where an arch pierced the wall.

"Huh! Huh! Huh!" they chanted.

Slowly the maypoles shortened. The platforms supporting them lowered into the earth beneath the trapdoors. *Good.* The theater for Sol's anniversary spectacle was set. Time to check on the feast.

A flicker of movement in the grove adjacent to the performance space caught Mercurio's eye. Were the cupbearers setting the viands forth already?

He bounded back down the massive blocks of the watching place, enjoying the change of perspective, the banked stones rising behind him.

Silenus, chief of the satyrs, touched Mercurio's shoulder before he could escape to the banquet grove. "Mea numen" – my deity – "the seat cushions can't be found anywhere." His tone was blunt, despite the honorific. "Have the Themeides not finished their work?"

Mercurio grimaced. These preparations had featured one glitch after another, but he'd plowed through all of them. He'd undoubtedly plow through this one as well, but . . . Cronos! Couldn't some aspect of the thing go smoothly?

"Semetra sent word that even the ornate bolster for Sol himself was complete a Gaian sevenday ago. Haven't the Melissae fetched them?"

Silenus spat, a nasty wad of saliva splatting on the clean white orchestra terrace. "Nope."

Mercurio frowned, then frowned more pointedly.

Silenus reddened and pulled a square of linen from the bandolier crossing his hairy chest. He bent and wiped the stone dry. Crumpled cloth in hand, he bowed. "Beg forgiveness, mea numen."

"You have it."

Mercurio sharpened the curtness in his voice. "Don't let it happen again. Gaia herself will grace this celebration. Artemis Diana, Proserpina, Star, and Juno as well. And they are not the greatest of the guests. Sol himself will step on this rock, sit upon it. Treat it accordingly."

"Yes, mea numen." Silenus shuffled his hooves, clattering them in his unease. "But the cushions?"

"Send the Boucolai" – the pastoral nymphs – "to

bring them here. Gaia has seen that it will not rain before the spectacle begins."

"Yes, mea numen!" Silenus cantered abruptly away.

Mercurio's lips stretched in a grin. Satyrs. Never civilized, but clever. And knew how to organize anything from a bacchanalia to an impromptu romp. Useful for an occasion like this.

He bounced once on his toes, then strode across the orchestra, noting that the trap doors lay perfectly flat and smooth. None of his performers would trip.

The path to the banquet grove was narrow and winding, smooth beaten earth between pillows of turf. Had he been right to leave it in its natural state? A paved path might be more convenient, but the goddesses would enjoy the pastoral beauty of the less manicured way. *I'll summon nymphs and satyrs to escort anyone who grows too inebriated to negotiate the passage,* he decided.

In the banquet grove, sunlight passed through the rounded leaves of the old olive trees to dapple the space charmingly. The savory aroma of roasting meats drifted on its still air, and a trio of nymphs, barely visible through the rough-barked trunks, bustled among the padded benches intended for the lesser guests.

Ganymede, flaunting a bit too much youthful thigh beneath his short copper-bordered tunic, skipped into the triclinium formed by the couches for the greater guests. He bore an armful of white lilies, which he presented to Hebe. She laughed and shook her head, gesturing with the tray from which she was serving pale pats of ambrosia – herbed chevre – onto each of the nine places at the rightmost of two low, square tables.

"Give them to Lixy," she directed. "I've got my hands full."

Immersed in her chosen vocation, serving the greater celestials and planetaries, Hebe glowed with pleasure. Her ivory complexion and honey-gold hair, bound up by electrum bands, shone warm and radiant. She'd chosen soft peach tones for her peplos and stola to accentuate her flushed beauty. And, ordinarily, Mercurio would appreciate her loveliness with the concentration of a connoisseur.

But, today, he noticed her only as a foil for Lixy.

Where Hebe glowed, Lixy blazed, her milky skin alight as though the sun's rays burst from her core rather than from Sol above. Her brunette tresses, elaborately braided and secured by platinum bands, held a dark radiance unusual to their curling strands. Her peplos and stola, a pale, pale azure bordered with more platinum, seemed to burn with the effulgence of a blue gas giant. Through the translucent silk, her lithe curves beckoned.

Mercurio felt his breath grow short.

Alluring upon his first glimpse of her, so many months ago, Lixy's charm had only grown as she recovered her health. He scrutinized her a moment. Was she well? Their journey through the void between the second and fourth spheres had drained her slightly. Nothing like the low ebb at her arrival in his demesne, but worrisome nonetheless.

Sunbathing in the amphitheater had restored her, and she'd left him to his last-minute spectacle-organizing tasks, while she hurried to join Ganymede and Hebe in last-minute banquet-arranging.

Now she accepted Ganymede's armful of lilies and bent to distribute them in the urns surrounding Proserpina's *kline*, the angled couch on which the goddess would recline, head toward the table, feet away from it.

Straightening, Lixy noticed Mercurio paused at the grove's edge and flashed him a heartstopping grin before crossing to his side.

"We swapped the Haden-Minerva-Ares trio with the Neptunus-Ceres-Saturnus trio," she informed him. "Ganymede pointed out that while Juno tolerates Haden and Minerva, she's angry with her son Ares right now. Best not to provoke her wrath by having him right around the corner from her!"

Ah, yes. Developing a seating plan for the greater immortals at a feast was tricky at best, sometimes impossible.

They numbered a perfect eighteen for the proper configuration – twice nine – but settled hatreds and rivalries meant only a few arrangements worked. And more ephemeral disagreements – such as this between Ares and Juno – could disrupt even those.

Juno and Star must be kept as far from one another as possible.

Star required a personable male at hand.

Ceres would bear her father Saturnus with well-bred ease, but could not abide her grandfather Ouranos.

Mercurio had derived what he thought the perfect plan until he realized that excluding Lixy from the banquet was no longer acceptable to him. But where to place a nineteenth seat? Perhaps he could give up his own to her and join the cupbearers in their serving duties? But that would insult Sol – to not partake in the meal – and require him to find someone other than himself to amuse Star.

When he'd brought the problem to Gaia, she'd suggested Lixy sit at her side, on the corner around from Haden.

"Sol's ceremonial space measures so broad that, even with Juno and I flanking him, there's plenty of room for a fourth." She nodded firmly. "And I'd be delighted to get better acquainted with your guest!"

Problem solved.

But Ganymede was quite right about Juno and Ares. Mercurio had forgotten that Juno was furious because Ares had refused her proffered babysitting services for his latest offspring, the quadruplets Eros, Antero, Himer, and Potho. Nor was she best pleased that their mother was Star. Good catch!

Ganymede bustled back into the grove with a fresh bowl of pomegranate seeds. The chevre pats on the one table already possessed their vivid, jeweled frames of pips. The other table was about to receive its share.

"Let me help with that," Mercurio insisted, reaching for Ganymede's bowl. He would need to don his formal garb soon, but there was time for this.

The youth nodded, relinquished the pomegranates, and sped away to his next task.

Lixy fetched Stargazer lilies – ivory bespeckled with magenta – with which to adorn Star's *kline*. Hebe departed to check on the nymphs' progress in cooking the kebabs featured in the first course.

Mercurio began arraying the pomegranate pips in starburst patterns on the plates. First Plurima, then Vulcanus, then Artemis Diana.

He glanced over his shoulder.

Oh, good. Lixy was done with Star's flowers and moving on to those of Ceres, golden-hued lilies.

He lounged casually over to the three *klinia* opposite those where he'd just finished.

Pip, pip, pip for Ouranos.

And now . . . he slipped the brass wallet tucked beneath his belt into his hand. It felt cool to his touch.

"Mercurio?" called Lixy from where she fussed with Ceres' blooms. "Do you think I should add a sheaf of wheat to the bouquet for Ceres? If I put some yellow gladiolus in too, it won't clash."

Mercurio pushed the wallet into a fold of his tunic and turned.

Lixy was holding up the combination she envisioned, a rich cluster of varying deep yellows.

"Perfect!" he allowed, turning away only when Lixy bent again to her task.

Quickly he pulled the wallet from its concealment and opened it.

The three pips he'd carried away from Haden glistened like drops of blood, vibrant and beguiling. He tipped them into his hand, stowed the wallet under his belt again, and deliberately placed the tainted seeds: here, here, and here. Proserpina would taste these, even if she ignored the rest.

Mercurio bit his lip. And moved on to serve his own plate.

"Ganymede!" Hebe had returned. "Hurry! The celestials approach!"

Lixy shifted her weight from her right foot to her left and sipped sparkling nectar from a slender crystal flute. White grape, Hebe had said. It prickled on her tongue, sharp and invigorating.

Such a different taste from the mellow ciders of home.

She glanced around the grove, enjoying the more golden light of this system's primary and the graceful foliage of the fourth sphere.

The mingled perfumes of the flowers around the dining couches tickled her nose. Would they make her sneeze when everyone finally sat? The green hydrangeas adorning her *kline* reminded her of the lace-cups of home.

So strange that she could remember so much of Helicon – its whiter light and umbrella trees, the names and personalities of her attendants, what Phrosyne said that time she tripped on Lixy's sandal – but she couldn't remember the most important thing: their significance. How did she fit into that milieu, and what were her responsibilities?

She shook her head, more a jerk of her chin than a real shake, and returned her attention to Ares.

The guardian of Mars stood slightly taller than Mercurio, but his physique was burlier. Handsome, of course, as were all Sol's court: tightly curling black hair, pale olive skin, firm and clean-shaven chin, and keen gray eyes. Right now he puffed out his chest and gestured, his crimson toga swirling with the motion as he described his wrestling match against the constellation Herakles.

"In the end it was a draw," he admitted, his grin deprecating. Then his eyes brightened. "But Herakles, you know! Or, I guess you don't. But no one even ties him, let alone bests him."

"It sounds exciting," murmured Lixy. "I wish I'd seen it."

Ares' glance brightened still more. "We could

arrange a re-match. Herakles would relish the chance to defeat me soundly. What do you say to next transition?"

But at that moment Star drifted up, Basileus on her arm.

"Lixy, darling, the mightiest of Sol's planetaries is longing to chat with you. You mustn't let Ares monopolize your charms!" And she bore her lover away.

Really, everyone had been most kind. Even the guardian of Venus, once Star recognized that Lixy's coloring and garb complemented her own red tresses and cloth-of-gold peplos and stola rather than competing with them.

This gathering was fun. Lixy smiled up at Basileus.

Another virile immortal, although in a more majestic style, bearded and looming. He captured her free hand and drew it to his lips in a formal salute.

"My lady, welcome to Sol's demesne. Have you taken pleasure in your visit among us? Is Mercurio hosting you properly?" His brows quirked faintly, as though he doubted Mercurio could host anyone properly. "I shouldn't think there's much to see in that strange clockwork mansion of his."

She assured him that she found Mercury's orbit fascinating. Which was true, no matter how unlikely Jupiter's guardian found it.

"But you must visit the sixth sphere for an interval, as well. Juno and I would love to entertain you in our court. Our players are second to none, our table, always graced with Hebe's best efforts, and our pleasure grounds, extensive. You must come!"

Somehow she felt reluctant. It would be dimmer there, surely, so far from this system's primary. And . . . she'd miss Mercurio. But how did one politely decline the invitation of a king?

"Thank you, majesty. Perhaps you might present me to your lady queen?" Would that distract him?

And it seemed it would. He bowed and proffered his arm. She placed her hand above his wrist and moved with him toward Juno.

Ganymede approached them, a pyramid of plums, their skins so purple as to seem black, weighing his tray. "Do taste one," he urged. "They're luscious!"

When Lixy declined, the cupbearer turned away.

Basileus drew her onward, and she stumbled.

He steadied her.

They both scrutinized the lawn for whatever had caught her left foot. Ah, one of Ganymede's plums had fallen. How dark and sullen it looked, there on the sun-bright grasses.

"Oh!" broke from Lixy's lips.

Her escort bent his head toward her in concern. "My lady? You are ill?"

Had her face paled? She felt like it had. "No, no. I'm well," she insisted. And she was, but . . . oh! A snippet of memory had returned. A memory that was . . . weighty, important . . . significant.

"You *are* ill. Let me summon the nymphs," suggested Basileus, his arm firm beneath her palm, his other hand atop hers. "They will minister to you."

"No. I'm well. I just –"

Oh, if only Mercurio were here at her side. He would understand. She could explain to him. But how could she make Basileus realize that returning memory could startle one so much, when he didn't know that she'd lost any memory to require returning. She felt her fingers trembling.

And then Mercurio *was* there, guiding her to a *kline* – her *kline* – where she could sit, persuading Basileus to leave them, shielding her from the notice of the rest.

He knelt before her, her hands in his. "Lixy, what happened?"

"'Curio, I remembered!"

His hands tightened. "Good! Tell me! Unless . . ." he paused, "you'd rather not." His eyes met hers anxiously. "You're well, Lixy?"

Surely *he* knew she wasn't ill. Didn't he?

"Of course, I'm well! And, of course, I'll tell you! I only remembered a bit, but it feels like the root of everything."

He searched her face, reached out one arm toward Hebe – who was suddenly and smoothly there – and selected a morsel of persimmon from the cupbearer's tray.

"I think you need this," he told her, holding the fruit before her lips. She opened them, accepting his offering. Sweet, tangy flavor flooded her mouth. She chewed and swallowed. Under her, the cushioned surface felt firmer, as did the turf beneath her sandals. Perhaps the shock *had* weakened her.

"*Now* tell me," Mercurio instructed her.

"'Curio, I fell!"

His free hand rushed back to its fellow to grip hers.

"Just now? I didn't see. Are you hurt?"

She couldn't help laughing. Gentle laughter.

"No, not now. When I left home. Just as I was starting out. Not really fell, because I was translating from sphere to sphere, like you do here. But my left ankle collided with something, hard. It bounded away from me, I saw it, dark and –" she shook her head, a real head shake this time "– and I plunged headlong, tumbling wildly."

She could hear the excitement in her voice.

"I think I fainted. Or something. Because the next thing I knew, I was in space strange to me, a void between nameless stars, and wandering. I kept going, but I was lost. It grew ever darker and colder. And I became afraid." She shivered. "I went on and on."

There was a haunting memory.

"And then I came to your Mercury." She smiled. "And blessed warmth."

His arm was around her shoulders now, his side warm against hers, a fold of his amber toga enfolding her. Silly to keep shaking, really.

"Sh," he whispered. "Sh. It's over now. You're here, and you're safe."

"Yes." She felt safe.

And welcome. "Yes, I am." And happy.

"Thank you, Mercurio." It was for far more than his current comfort, but he seemed to know that. His arm pulled her close.

The bright call of a horn rang out. Golden notes going up and up, then a final sonorous blare.

Mercurio raised his head. "It's Sol! Can you stand?"

In the great dark, Draco coursed, riding the wave homeward, glorying in its power.

The void beyond the Oort Cloud had taken him years to traverse.

He sensed the Teleio Mauro had already pushed him farther in moments than he'd flown in months.

The current roared in his celestial senses, fast and dense and furious, scented like a mix of anise and cold ice. He tightened the tension in his wings, clipped to his sides. The strength of this surf could break him, were he extended to its reach. Narrow and sinuous was the way to go, gliding on a stream like no other he'd known.

The sparkle of the outer Oort burst abruptly across the blackness, rushing upon him like snow blown by a blizzard, except that he was the storm here.

The flakes swelled from sparks to crystals to great spheres of ice and dust, each with its winged guardian. Praying no more, the spirit of the comet leapt upright when the dark wave tumbled her charge, face ecstatic and wings extended, not broken, but streaking sunward in a blaze of light, extravagant tail splashing the night. Hundreds of them wakening into splendor and racing through the void.

Draco felt the pressure at his own two scaly tails growing, mounting higher, more dense, more ferocious.

The scintillation of comets became a hail, a torrent.

Could Sol sense the flashing display where he flamed, far inside the inner Oort?

This was worthy of the primary, worthy of his birth from stardust, worthy of his birth's anniversary.

Draco grinned, there at the back of this cascade of light, imagining what Mercurio would say of his contribution to Sol's spectacle.

Hah! You begged me to perform, little planetary. How's this?

And then, amidst his triumph, Draco's satisfaction faltered.

What do I bring? Behind the brilliance, after the brilliance, what follows me and drives me?

A blackness dark enough, dense enough, mammoth enough to swallow . . . everything.

Draco spasmed, and the Teleio Mauro's shockwave took him, wrenching his great wings, cracking his long spine.

In pain, he tumbled.

Mercurio's arm beneath her elbow, Lixy rose to her feet.

Around them, the conversations of the planetaries fell silent as they turned to face an archway formed by the boughs of two oaks. Not the gap between a pair of olives where the path leading to the amphitheater began, and where a satyr stood stock still. Where Lixy and Mercurio had entered themselves.

The oaks framed a grander entrance proper to guests, where the planetaries and their retinues had arrived.

The leaves of the grove rustled in the breeze. The lesser celestials, scattered through the farther reaches of the banquet space, sang a brief high note, clear and without words.

The air stilled and grew warmer. An aroma of honey spiced with pepper lapped the gathering. The sunlight shining through the twin oaks intensified into gold.

Sol stepped through the arch.

Lixy's breath caught.

Were beauty to clothe itself in masculine form,

were strength to coalesce into clean limbs and a quick-moving stride, were love to wear a lover's face, then they three shone incarnate in Sol.

His garb was more plain than that of all his celebrants, a simple short tunic, unadorned white. No crown encircled his curling golden hair. And yet majesty hung about him, a garment richer than the garnished silks worn by his court. His voice was deep and warm.

"I am come, beloved ones."

And delight beamed in his gaze.

"Hail, great Sol!" Lixy found herself joining in the chorus.

Who could deny this primary honor? She wished he was hers. Who *was* the primary of Helicon? What a strange gap in her tattered memory.

Basileus bowed so low as Sol entered the grove that his knee touched down. Sol raised him, and saluted each cheek. "Princepsus Basileus Fortescue, I am blessed in you. Steady, well judging, and discerning. Be always yourself." Did Basileus redden?

Juno's courtesy dipped equally low. Sol's face softened as he raised her.

Lixy wanted to turn to Mercurio. To ask him . . . something. To tell him . . . something else. To express her amazement and see if he shared it.

But Sol riveted her attention. She could not look away from him.

And then he stood before her, warmer than sunlight, though he was the sun; mightier than divinity, though he was divine; and focused only on her.

She felt her knees start to fold. His hands caught her wrists before she sank to her courtesy.

"Never to me, my lady, no. I am honored by your presence, most radiant. Veloxus looks high for my guests." The weight of his awareness glanced aside, briefly, in an amused smile for Mercurio. Then it returned to her.

"Illustria Domina Claria" – bright lady of light – "speak your slightest wish while you tarry here with us, and it shall be yours."

He bowed to her. Then passed on.

She felt breathless and exhilarated all at once. Relieved from the pressure of his glance, longing for its return. Sol's was no easy presence to bear.

She began to find her balance as he moved away from Mercurio, greeting each of his well-wishers with his full attention and appreciation.

She was grateful that Gaia would buffer her from Sol when they sat for the feast. *What if I had him immediately on my right?* Eating would be impossible.

Conversing . . . more so.

Lixy turned at last to Mercurio. He looked as suffocated as she'd felt a moment ago.

"Is your primary always this overpowering?" she asked.

His eyes followed Sol through his court, then returned to hers. He nodded mutely, then found his voice. "You get used to it after a bit. Instead of pressing at you, it fills you up. You'll see."

She couldn't imagine it. And then, suddenly, she could.

Like those long hours in Mercurio's conservatory, soaking up sunlight. That was Sol, after all, if at more distance. This was Sol up close. And he felt equally good. Her shoulders relaxed, followed by the rest of her.

Which was fortunate.

When Mercurio led her to her dining couch, Gaia met her there to offer Lixy her own.

"Sol would do you honor," insisted Gaia, "and I find I concur."

Sol himself guided her onto Gaia's *kline*, his radiant hand warm beneath her elbow.

Mercurio reclined on his right side, trying to ignore Proserpina behind him, his face toward Star around the corner of the low table.

Bronze roses, stems wrapped in cinnamon bark, flanked his couch. Their scent – sweet spiked with spice – should have made him feel right at home. They didn't. Ditto the comfortable cushions of his *kline*, and the perfect incline of its slope, propped up at the table, slanting down at the foot.

How could he feel ease?

While . . . Proserpina still sipped her nectar while chatting amiably with Ouranos.

"Left your tongue at home with 'Gilem?" teased Star, one eyebrow delicately arched.

How strange that she should echo Draco's words from the start of this anniversary adventure.

Mercurio pulled himself together. He occupied this corner purely to amuse Star, so amuse her he must.

"Fox in the sunlight and apple on the tree, grant me sharp silver from your secret sheath."

A delicious ripple of laughter broke from Star's lips.

"You're incorrigible," she told him. "Why would a lady conceal a blade about her person? 'Tis the lord who wields the stave."

Her sidelong glance conveyed both her own innuendo and her understanding of his. But Mercurio had never underestimated Star's quickness. Unlike some.

"I would you wind me in your tresses, warm and close."

More laughter. "And how shall a lady's keenness encourage warmth? *Her* tongue? Surely not!" Another melting look assured him that she didn't have her sharp wit in mind. "Lords shrivel under feminine fire, unless the fire be innate and mute."

"My aim is too practical to be worthy of your ear."

"Oh?" Her smile hinted secrets. "Aims and ears hold promise."

Indeed, hers were beautiful, curving shells of ivory, but he wished he were bantering with Lixy. Except Lixy's humor was more genuine and less self-centered than Star's. Less jaded.

I wish she reclined around the corner from me.

He repressed a sigh.

The lesser guests were drifting through the farther reaches of the grove to their couches. A lingering nymph cast a coquettish peek over her shoulder at the satyr waiting there. Half the greater celestials, here in the main triclinium, remained standing. Mercurio wished Basileus would settle. He'd engage Star's attention when he did, and Mercurio could use a break. About now.

"My aim has thievish propensities."

At least he could carry on like this almost in his sleep. And convincingly. Star (or any other lady) would never guess his heart wasn't in it.

Footsteps approached behind him. Hebe? Or one of her nymphs? The tread was too deliberate, too heavy. He sensed someone looming.

Star's eyes widened. Somehow Mercurio didn't think it was because of his latest sally, but she ignored whoever it was.

"But do you marry thievish thoughts with persuasive ones?" she asked.

"For you, nothing else. My tongue is silver."

"Silver again?" she lilted. "But not sharp this time? And not mine?"

"Oh, yours and mine. Yours, sharp. Mine, smooth to find your sharpness."

And now Basileus did recline. Laughing, Star turned to him.

Mercurio looked over his shoulder to see who stood there.

Great Cronos! It was Haden, cooly surveyed by his wife.

"You should be pleased with the first course," Proserpina informed him.

She wasn't looking at Mercurio, but Mercurio winced and wished he hadn't lent himself to Haden's schemes. Did Haden flinch as well? If so, it was internally. His toga, black velvet, hung without a ripple.

His voice, in reply, sounded distant. "It pleases me not at all."

What was he doing here?

Mercurio had made considerable effort to be sure Haden and Proserpina dined on the same side of the tables where they could not see one another, and with Ouranos, Ares, and Minerva separating them.

"Perhaps I do you injustice." Was that sadness crossing Proserpina's face. She plucked a pomegranate pip from her plate and brought it toward her lips.

Haden's silence chilled the air around him.

"Once I loved pomegranate." Proserpina studied the pip held so close to her mouth.

Mercurio held his breath.

Haden shifted, ever so slightly. "What justice would you visit upon me, queen of shadow?"

Abruptly Proserpina replaced the pip on her plate, rising to a sitting position. "Don't call me that!"

Haden bowed and stretched out his right arm toward the edge of the grove where Hebe waited. The cupbearer approached, tray in hand.

Proserpina slid her legs around, the dark ivory silk of her peplos rustling with the movement, so that she could perch at the head of her *kline*.

Almost defiantly, she collected the pomegranate pip again and placed it in her mouth.

Haden bent swiftly to kiss her.

Great and little goddesses!

Proserpina tried to pull away, then submitted when Haden's hand behind her head constrained her. He prolonged the kiss to quite improper length.

His lower lip dripped red when he drew away.

Had she bit him?

No, it was pomegranate juice.

Suddenly Mercurio twigged to what was really transpiring here. And thus was not surprised when Haden swiped the dish holding an apricot half, sauced with sweet cream, from Hebe's tray. And swapped it for Proserpina's plate, untouched save the one pip that *Haden – not* Proserpina – had swallowed.

Proserpina's look of outrage transformed to one of wonder.

Haden bowed again, waited for Hebe to serve

Mercurio, and then turned on his heel to go. He did not see Proserpina's hand, reaching to stay him.

Mercurio tightened his fists and looked away, staring unseeing at Star's graceful back.

What a mess! That was the last time he ever interfered between husband and wife.

And it wasn't really Haden's scheme. *It was* mine, *proposed to fit* my *plans, pushed against Haden's better instincts.* Where else had he erred in the push to get his way?

At his back, Proserpina's voice recalled his attention.

"It's not your fault, Mercurio," she said.

He rose to match her sitting posture. "It *is* my doing. I suggested it. I supervised it. I carried it through." Did she even realize the doom she'd just dodged?

"I knew what came to me."

So she did realize. Then why . . . ?

"Haden and I will join hands in time. I'd hoped this might be a short cut, but I was wrong to so use my husband's weakness. The long way round . . . must suffice. As I should know."

Like Star's, her smile – sad – held a secret, but a secret utterly different from her aunt's. It scared him, and beckoned him too.

Dazzling streaks of brightness laced the darkness as Draco tumbled, and the pain went on and on, throbbing in his twin tails, stabbing his kinked spine, and burning his shredded wings.

It will never end, he realized.

This wave that shook him loomed larger than Sol's demesne, larger than the Oort Cloud, larger – perhaps – than the vast distances between star and star. If he waited for it to release him, for his wounded body to tumble loose from its grasp, the way a pebble in white water might bound free to a place of rest, it would never happen.

What can I do?

It was hard to think with the cosmos spinning dizzily around him and the wrongness in his broken body pressing him. Was endurance his only option?

The dry, thin nothing smell of the Oort threaded through the chilling anise of the Teleio Mauro. It steadied his thoughts even while the rest of him continued its wild plummet.

That's not the smell of nothing, he recognized. It's the echo of energy so contained it *resembles* nothingness. Had he senses properly attuned, he suspected it would sizzle or hiss.

A stronger buffet flung his two tails asunder. The sheer agony of the unnatural split whited out his awareness for a moment.

Aagh!

If only he were a planetary, not a mere celestial, and a constellation at that.

Mercurio has a choice, burn him! Whether to soar on his sandals or translate from sphere to sphere.

Translation was no faster, but it rendered the traveler less vulnerable to the conditions around him. Could Mercurio translate here? The guardian of the inmost planet grew chilled in the outer reaches of Sol's demesne. Had he ever left Sol's heliosphere, gone beyond the heliopause? Draco thought not.

What would it be like, translating from the outer Oort to the inner, from the inner Oort to the Kuiper Belt, and from there to Haden's realm?

Draco felt himself stretching as he imagined it, stretching and waxing gossamer, as though the tidal forces tossing him blew through his bones instead of against them. Larger and larger he stretched, thinner and thinner he waned.

What was happening?

Did the Teleio Mauro probe forward with yet another evil?

No, this was something belonging specially to Draco, something never imagined, something never . . . needed.

Draco *stretched*, and stretched again.

His pain faded.

He grew larger than Sol, larger than the heliopause, larger even than the Oort. How was this possible?

Then he knew and felt foolish.

Of course.

His essence anchored in a pattern of stars seen in Gaia's night sky. It possessed no inherent size. He was all a matter of perspective.

How had he forgotten?

He'd known himself long ago, when Sol was young, before Gaia herself was born, when Draco partook of a child's joy.

When had he grown so jaded that the early memories palled?

Draco stretched again: larger than the void between Sol and Proxima Centauri, larger than the Proxume Sphaera, the "local bubble" in which Sol and his neighbors swung.

And now he could see it.

A vast irradiated orb, its center darker than dark,

its halo glowing hot purples and hotter blues: the Teleio Mauro kicked loose by Semotus and Umbra, traversing the journey from the galaxy's heart to this farflung spiral arm where Sol dwelt.

Draco turned from home and dove outward, almost invisible in his transparency, streaking faster than a comet.

Lixy studied the sky. Its soft turquoise had deepened, the way it did with evening's advent, shading down toward the horizon through cream, pale yellow, and a broad band of deep gold. Sol's sun was setting behind the proscenium.

It was beautiful, a necklace of light encircling the fourth sphere, casting rich radiance over the folded green mountains, the stone of the amphitheater, and the vivid silks of the celestials seated on the curving banked tiers.

With the nymphs, constellations, and satellites congregated around the greater immortals, they made a resplendent crowd. Their perfumes – warm sandalwood, cool cucumber, and spicy amber – mingled with the faint aroma of woodsmoke rising from the kitchen fires on the far side of the banquet grove. Late supper would be served close on midnight.

Lixy sighed and adjusted her position slightly, feeling hard stone beneath her press against her thighs. She could have had a cushion. Sol had ushered her to his own firm bolster. And she'd declined. Politely, reminding him that he must not neglect his longtime friends for a newcome guest, however much she enjoyed the honor.

A puzzled look had crossed his noble face.

"All my honor could not suffice you, my lady, but you are right to value old acquaintance."

And he'd allowed her to move away from him.

She'd chosen this spot at the amphitheater's edge, a little distance away from the others, unsure why she wanted solitude. But she did.

Something was changing within her, and she wanted to sort it out.

When had the change begun?

So hard to tell. She'd been changing ever since she started her journey. From . . . some state unknown to her to lost and . . . dying? Then from cold and weak to welcomed and convalescing.

Her lips curved, remembering Mercurio's first hospitality: so discombobulated he'd been, but – at heart – kind.

She'd become an increasing partner in Mercurio's aims and milieu, until her participation and attendance at Sol's festivity seemed a given. And then she'd stumbled on that fallen plum. *That* was the change she wanted to pinpoint: that alteration in her awareness.

What had produced it?

For the plum was irrelevant in itself. A mere trigger for a deeper reality.

Her memory of her fall through the cosmos was the important bit. That and her sense that some lost part of her was returning, translating through nested spheres from great distance, through her outermost aura as it approached.

Who would she be when it penetrated through her inner spheres to the core essence at her heart?

She still didn't know.

But I'll be finding out soon. The change was accelerating rather than diminishing.

She considered the heavens again.

Had something changed there as well? Was the sunlight more concentrated, more intense, more golden? Like its illuminating rays that pierced more strongly through leaf and grass blade as the sun dropped lower toward the horizon? Like that, but somehow different?

The turquoise dome overhead had darkened to cobalt, and the highest band of cream, turned dusky. The lowest band, still gold, blazed. Was it merely sunset, beautiful, but expected?

I think it's something else.

She was not the only one studying the sky. Others in the audience were noticing . . . something.

Not Sol, or his immediate retinue, whose attention very properly focused on the stage below. But Hebe leaned in worriedly toward Ganymede, whispering, agitated, and gesturing. A cluster of satyrs rose from their seats and climbed to the amphitheater's highest tier behind Lixy, their hooves clattering on the stone.

Would the higher vantage yield them more information?

Should she join them?

Do I need more information? No. All she needed was right here. Right inside her.

How do I feel? The celestials were troubled, uneasy, their mood spreading through the gathering. Even Basileus and Juno looked tense, although they clapped politely as the trio of tightrope walkers took their bows.

Am I worried?

No, she wasn't.

I feel strong.

When had that started? At the banquet? With the fallen plum?

No, not then.

Nor when she'd sat at Sol's side, speaking to him of the wonders she'd discovered in his second sphere – Mercurio's sphere – and hearing, in turn, of the special beauties offered by the other planetaries. Gaia had told her a funny story about Pan and his panpipes. And then there'd been the brief interval when Sol attended his other dinner partner, Juno on his right side, and when Gaia conversed with Haden on her left.

Lixy had watched Mercurio flirting with Star.

He was very convincing. And yet *she* wasn't convinced.

She didn't think Star – who clearly expected male admiration – was disappointed. But despite his gallant efforts, Mercurio's heart wasn't in it. Strange, since he enjoyed the company of a beautiful woman. And Star was lovely.

I wonder what he's looking for, that Star does not possess?

And then there'd been that bizarre incident between Proserpina and Haden. Lixy didn't know their story, but their brief confrontation radiated fraught emotion.

The course of the banquet was leisurely, featuring many elaborate dishes – roast peacock and jellied eels and more – interspersed with performances by musicians and dancers and breaks for the guests to stroll the grove and converse with those seated elsewhere.

Always Lixy was accompanied by Sol or Neptunus or one of the greater immortals, almost as though *she* rather than Sol were being celebrated.

Did they know something about her that she didn't know herself?

No. They did not.

It was Sol. Sol knew . . . something. And the rest took their tone from him.

I should ask him!

She half rose, then sank back. No. The answers lay within. And she needed her own knowledge, not someone else's.

She continued tracing the afternoon in her memory, trying to locate the moment when her intimation of change had become change itself.

Had it been when they traversed the path from the banquet grove to the amphitheater? Star had required the attendants Mercurio summoned, though she chose two nymphs to support her rather than the male oreads who offered themselves longingly. And despite the goddess' uncertain footsteps, she retained her splendor and her dignity.

Ouranos, too, required help. *He* chose three nymphs, leering repulsively and fondling them as they steered him. Ugh! Lixy wasn't sure why she felt laughter in her throat with that memory instead of disgust, but she did.

The start of the spectacle had been . . . spectacular!

Accompanied by a fanfare of trumpets, Sagittarius and his cohort of archers strode onto the stage on stilts shaped like fauns' legs. Their silver hose and vests glittered in the bright sun. Their arrows blazed with a cold lilac fire.

And the patterns created by their shots – a continuous stream of missiles, crisscrossing, spraying high, and bending in an unfelt wind – made a dazzling filigree of light, ever shifting as the archers varied their angles of aim and the phosphorescence passed through the full spectrum from violet to blue and green, then on through gold, amber, and crimson.

It ended in a vibrant magenta fountain and a sudden massed shout from the archers.

Magnificent!

Lixy found herself on her feet clapping without realizing she'd stood.

But the change she'd sensed in herself had not come then.

Nor in any moments of the day before either.

There had been no discrete switch from *not this* to *this*. Just the long painful waning of her travels and her gradual convalescence under Mercurio's protection, blending into her increasing well-being and strength.

She turned from her inward concentration to the current performers.

They deserved attention: a charming confusion of doleful clowns, Saturnus' jesters, skillfully doing apparently inadvertent slapstick, falling down to get up and tumble a neighbor, turning around to tip another, and crying all the while.

In mid-act, they were not finished, but Lixy stood anyway.

She had to stand. The energy growing within her demanded it.

Her arms rose as though to embrace the sky, and her face tipped up. A geyser of jubilation fizzed through her.

I am strong. I am whole. I am!

Mercurio paused where he stood on the very edge of the stage.

The gas lamps – his own contribution, not the satyrs' – lit the performers brilliantly in the gathering dusk, but the shadows under the adjacent oaks grew dense. He doubted the audience could see him. Flickering lanterns on the amphitheater steps, much dimmer than the stage lights, picked out a jutting beard here, wide eyes there, parted lips, a wondering face.

I've done it. I've succeeded. Sol himself is amazed.

Mercurio turned back to the stage.

All seven clowns had pulled the triggers inflating their purple and silver costumes into balls. With clever gymnast tricks, each rolled head over heels, round and round, bouncing against one another. Amazing the things a satyr could accomplish with stiff wire.

There'd been a dicey moment at the end of the tightrope act before the clowns.

The quick-release for the cable suspended between the two maypoles failed to function. The satyrs, pumping away at the cranks to retract the poles, hadn't noticed, and the braided metal would have fouled the trap doors for sure. Luckily Mercurio *had* noticed. It had been an easy thing to fly on his sandals' wings and detach the wire manually.

He glanced at the sky. Where were the stars? Venus should be hanging low and radiant against the deepening blue. The northern cross of Cygnus, soaring in the higher dome.

Mercurio frowned.

What was that peculiar flatness obscuring the evening's splendor?

There should be greater intensity as vivid ultramarine shaded into velvety indigo and then shining black. An increasing sense of the vast distances of the cosmos.

Not this deadening opacity.

Mercurio shut his eyes, the better to open his celestial perceptions.

Dull sable nothingness pressed against him, dry and thin and unpromising. It had no depth, and yet it took up space. Length and width and heighth. He extended himself into it.

What *was* this?

A flare of ultraviolet slashed the lifeless black and coalesced into a ring, burning, corroding, acidic. Within the aching amethystine glow, a blacker black abided.

Oh, Cronos! Now he knew. It was the Teleio Mauro, brought here by Mercurio's agency.

And it brought nothing good.

Flying down the great dark, Draco prepared himself.

The Teleio Mauro's lurid halo of searing blues and fiery violets intensified as he closed upon it. The black at its heart began to exert its pull, weighty and inexorable. Strength and might could never defeat it. What could?

Using Haden, I kicked this thing loose. Now it is mine to intercept.

Power would avail him nothing, but his lesson in perspective had given him the answer. Instead of pushing or exerting, he would open and receive.

Draco stretched yet again.

His twin tails reached the void between galaxy and galaxy. His jaws touched the penumbra of the singularity. Gah! It burned! Blistering his face.

He opened his maw.

And swallowed.

Agony blazed through his entrails and burst from his scaly hide.

Haden sat apart from his fellow planetaries, apart even from their retinue of lesser celestials. Perched on the amphitheater's uppermost tier just where the side steps ended, he frowned at the flickering lantern there. And extended a fastidious forefinger and thumb to pinch it out.

The flame scorched his skin for an instant, hot counterpoint to the cooling stone beneath his haunches.

He'd watched while the archers on stilts shot their missiles. While Bellatrix and her handmaidens balanced gracefully on the tightwire. While Saturnus' crying clowns made the audience laugh.

Charming. No doubt Gaia was pleased. Certainly Sol was.

Haden . . . was not.

He extended his celestial powers to bring up a phosphorescent glow upon the marble surrounding him, sickly green and tainted mauve.

The next act pleased him more.

Comet after comet blazed across the night sky, tails spread in splendor, vast sprays of refulgent light.

Outshining the stars and the planets. Outshining Gaia's shadow.

The applause was thin. Did the watching celestials sense that this was no deed of Mercurio's? That Haden's agency produced this shower of cometary delight?

Haden glanced to his right. What were the satyrs doing there opposite him, on the far end of the top tier? Clattering their hooves and murmuring and pointing. Who did they point to? Who was that figure standing below them?

Slight and pale and glowing white, she stood gazing upward, her attention rapt.

Mercurio's guest. The recipient of Sol's honor and respect. Who was she to inspire a primary's awe? Haden's eyes followed her focus toward the show above them.

A dragon soared the night sky, its scales limned in glowing blue, its jaws stretched wide to catch a black orb enrobed in ultraviolet malevolence.

Draco!

The constellation grew, twin tails touching one horizon, reaching foreclaw to stab the other.

His maw opened and opened.

And then swallowed the Teleio Mauro down.

His scales burst into flame, bright and golden, exuding dark, spiraling smokes.

"Oh!" cried the watching crowd. "A salamander!"

Draco raced from sight.

But the Teleio Mauro remained, swallowed, yet unswallowed, its darkness approaching to devour Sol's demesne.

Haden stood up.

Had he always known it would come to this? Perhaps not. If he'd known, he might have saved . . . much. But the coming challenge felt right.

The ninth sphere where Pluto swung in its far-flung orbit around Sol was hours of travel from Gaia's realm. Neither celestial translation nor a ride on Draco's back could get Haden there in time for action. But a planetary possessed an abiding link to his planet.

Always.

Haden closed his eyes and touched his foundation.

Cold stone and colder ice. A colossal pebble rolling around the solar system's rim, defining the heliopause, tracing an immense space-time disk.

Haden rooted himself in the phenomenon of his home. Deep in the bedrock, one with its mass, mighty in its essence. From that anchoring, he reached out past the heliopause, through the perturbed comets of the Oort Cloud, out into the void through which the Teleio Mauro approached.

The singularity burned, scorching the flesh from his fingers, revealing the white bones of his hands. He stifled the scream in his throat. And reached further, encircling the dark orb with his arms even as the flesh melted from them.

He stood revealed as a death lord complete, skeletal from skull to toe joint.

Then the black hole exerted its true power, claiming him for its own.

His bones stretched, pulled on the rack of impossible gravity. Pain, equally impossible, permeated his core and detached him, rootlet by rootlet, from his essence. He felt Pluto slide from his influence, slide from his touch. Then he plunged toward the ultraviolet-wreathed darkness, first expanded to the heighth of lightyears, then compressed to the minuteness of the *planck* length, smaller than an atom.

Soundless and sightless, he existed only as pain. Pain of every kind.

Fiery agony and frozen agony.

Suffocation.

Tortured expansion and tortured compression.

He died a million times over. All in an instant, yet on and on across an eternity.

Now he did scream. With no result, no resonance. Except as awareness, he did not exist. Except for his torture, he was nothing.

And then something changed.

His pain ebbed as though it had never been.

He floated in a sea of ease, whole, restored, and embodied.

He could feel his limbs, strong and robed in wholesome flesh. Languorous, and yet energized.

Then the darkness flashed into light, radiant and golden-white, too bright for even immortal eyes, but not too bright for his.

He saw a visage, beloved and familiar, yet utterly strange.

The divine mother of all wore Proserpina's face that he might recognize her and feel welcomed.

I am come home. Darkness was only my temporary haven, never my ultimate abode.

Haden welcomed his welcomer.

Dear Sol in his sphere!

Mercurio stood rooted to the spot, sheltered by the oaks at the stage's edge.

Stunned, he stared at Haden's transformations.

From the planetary's lesser form – masculine sublimity of modest stature – into his greater manifestation: a colossus of a being, crowned head piercing the sky to touch the stars, robe-shrouded feet plunged deep in the mire of the cosmos' foundations.

From vast immortal, transposed yet again, into death's image, a towering skeleton bearing absolute blackness in his bony hand.

Then the grim reaper stretched, impossibly extended from one edge of the galaxy to the other.

And he shattered.

A cloud of bone shards exploding outward, imploding inward, dissolving into dust, into nothing at all.

But the Teleio Mauro loured still, waxing in the comet-striped sky, an unstoppable threat.

Mercurio's limbs lost their horror-struck paralysis. Three bounds brought him from the proscenium to the amphitheater's lowest seats, and then he was leaping up the steps, dodging panicked celestials, ignoring Gaia's command to be calm.

Lixy's hands met his, warm and urgent.

"'Curio, I need you!"

Where Draco had failed, where Haden was destroyed, Mercurio could not succeed. But – by Sol himself! – if Lixy needed him, he would not fail *her*.

"Command me! Anything! I'm yours!"

"'Tis a little thing, 'Curio. So little you might think it unimportant and let it go. But you must not! All the galaxy depends upon it. Can you do it? No matter what comes?"

He had no doubt. None whatsoever.

Were she to transform as Haden had – but not, please Cronos, into oblivion like Haden – he would stand fast. Were she the cosmic serpent or primordial flame or a behemoth rising from the deeps, he would not let her go.

"Remember me! As I am to you now!" Tension edged her voice.

It was such a little thing. How could he ever forget?

"I promise," he vowed.

And then she changed.

First she brightened, her luminous person – dim in the dusk – growing radiant. Shedding beams of light – warm and golden in their essence, like Sol himself – but with a power within them, more edged, more cutting, almost blue-tinged and electric.

She far outshone the guttering lanterns on the stone steps and the stronger gas lamps trained on the stage. She lit the entire bowl of the amphitheater, creating daylight within its marble white confines.

Sol was standing, his back to the stage, gazing at Lixy. The greater immortals clustered around him, and the lesser around them, forming a clump of anxious watchers.

Then, like Haden, Lixy divested her lesser celestial form – womanhood perfected – for her greater manifestation.

But not like Haden. *Devouring light!*

Where Haden's crowned head brushed the nearer stars, Lixy's touched a neighboring galaxy, the Large Magellanic Cloud.

Potency rolled from her, a bone-shaking aura of force and intensity.

Sol's voice rose above the hubbub of his retinue: "Ulixia Chalcedonie Galaxias! *Numen* of the Milky Way, we honor you!"

Mercurio felt his breath puff out, like Sol had socked him in the stomach.

Cronos in chaos! He, a mere planetary, had been hosting the guardian of the Milky Way herself. He was not worthy.

She brightened yet again, the blue edges gaining on the golden heart, then shading over toward black.

Her aura intensified, moving from power into pain, a compression resembling that of the still approaching Teleio Mauro.

"'Curio!" Her voice buffeted him like a storm wind. How could it be so sweet and yet so strong? "Your promise! Please!"

Remembering her was impossible.

She was towering greatness, infinite sovereignty, the empress of every primary within her radius. *This* was who she was.

"'Curio!"

The desperation behind that sweet, wild call galvanized him. He had promised. But how could he make good on it? It seemed beyond him.

A cat's tail brushed his left shin.

Mercurio looked down to see Vigilem twining round his ankles. What in the solar system –?

"Clock winder, pick up your tools. This faltering becomes you not." The cat snickered.

His tools. Of course. Not the grippers and cutters and rivets he used in his gear-festooned hobby, the devising of clepsydra, no. Mercurio's real tools: the knowledge and will and decision he used to protect his planet and the celestial sphere it generated through him.

A planetary might be infinitely small when viewed against the galaxy, but his responsibility was real, and his powers – no matter how comparatively minute – real also.

Mercurio remembered.

Lixy, confused and alarmed in his bed chamber.

Lixy, pale and weak in the hall of clocks.

Lixy, warm and relaxed in his conservatory.

Lixy, engaged and interested in his spectacle for Sol.

Lixy, happy and energetic, while she prepared the celebratory dining grove beside this very amphitheater.

Lixy, supreme as she was now.

Ulixia Chalcedonie Galaxias. Herself in all manifestations. The lesser as much a part of her as the greater. Yes.

Mercurio remembered her. All of her.

Lixy felt the turbulence of the Large Magellanic Cloud's star nurseries blowing a loose tendril of her hair. Vast seas of hydrogen gas, glowing infrared, wreathed her head. A blaring supernova begemmed her brow. A necklace of white dwarfs adorned her neck.

I am whole.

I am huge.

I am!

She felt exultant. She felt brim full.

And, yet, she saw the small as well as the large.

The brilliant marble cup of the amphitheater cut into the side of one of Gaia's hills.

Sol, golden and glowing, gathering his flock of planetaries and celestials under his protection.

The bright silks and luxuriant velvets of the huddling retinue.

She saw them. And yet . . .

They *were* small. So small. They hardly held her attention.

More mesmerizing was the dense sphere of ultimate darkness, just there, before her outstretched hand. Heavy, alluring, robed in rings of throbbing ultraviolet.

It *called* her.

Ulixia! Seize me. Capture me. Fling me.

Feel my might.

Great as a galaxy. Great as thought.

Feel my destiny. Feel me devour!

Ah! She did feel it.

I will take it in my hand, the Teleio Mauro, and cast it into the void. See galaxies implode before it. See a universe bow.

And then she saw Mercurio, robed in his favorite amber, kneeling at her ankle.

Saw him and felt loss.

"'Curio! I need you! Please!"

Would he hear her? Would he help her? She could not do this alone.

He said nothing.

She stretched out her hand to the black hole.

Fierce was its energy, engulfing her palm.

And, yet, it was hers.

My heart. My essence. My anchor.

She gripped it, sorrowing for the deaths she would bring, rejoicing in the remembering of this piece of herself.

And then she felt Mercurio remembering Lixy.

Paralleling him, she remembered, too. Remembered *him.*

Mercurio, dazzled by her beauty.

Mercurio, hungry for her intimacies.

Mercurio, forbearing of her weakness.

Mercurio, nurturing her strength.

Mercurio, welcoming *her.*

"'Curio!" she cried. "*Wait* for me! The voids between star and star are too frigid for you. But I *will* come again to visit. That is my promise."

And then she claimed the Teleio Mauro.

Its violet ring burned, corrosive. Its black sphere weighed heavy, so heavy. Searing and devouring, it lay far beyond the control of any save a galactic.

Grasping it between her two hands, Lixy stopped it.

Holding it between her two palms, Lixy moved it.

Folding it to her breast, Lixy received it.

It disappeared within her core.

This is my heart. Dark power. Weighty creation. Mighty counterpart to her light.

And, yet, she was light.

As a light beam, she flew home. Bearing the Teleio Mauro with her to the center of the Milky Way.

The Pleiades were dancing on the amphitheater's stage, lit merely by Mercurio's limelights.

Connected by long elastic cords to the tops of the maypoles, they soared and twirled and linked arms in passing. Graceful and lovely, their offering to Sol – reverence and joy made into movement – brought an ache to Mercurio's heart.

Home was saved. Home was safe. Home was . . . home.

He sat at Sol's right hand and watched his planned spectacle conclude.

Modestly. Charmingly. Pleasingly.

And Sol was pleased.

There was a place for small pleasures. After a surfeit of magnificence, child-like enjoyment soothed and calmed.

Before the Pleiades had come the winged bulls and their fiery rings.

Before them too had performed the jugglers, the Simiae acrobats, and the contortionist.

The planetaries and the celestials and Sol himself had settled to their seats. The only remnant of their near destruction, the blaze of comets in the night sky.

All was well.

And, yet, Mercurio's heart ached.

The Pleiades took their bows. The satyrs retracted the maypoles one more time. And then an unplanned act unfolded. Genuine. Simple. Heartening.

"'Cur-i-o!"

"'Cur-i-o!"

"'Cur-i-o!"

The planetaries and their retinue were chanting Mercurio's name. *Lixy's* name for him. Sol raised him up and led him to the stage. The audience and the performers gathered around him and hoisted him to their shoulders, carrying him in a wide circular parade.

When, at last, they came to a standstill, Mercurio raised his arms and shouted, "Sol! All hail him! Sol!" And the crowd joined his salute.

Sol laughed.

"I've lost my ninth sphere and its planetary, but I've gained something precious, too. A true feeling of your loyalty, my children. Bless you each!"

And now Mercurio had more than knowing it. He felt it.

Lixy would visit.

All was well.

THE END

J.M. Ney-Grimm lives with her husband and children in Virginia, just east of the Blue Ridge Mountains. She's learning about permaculture gardening and debunking popular myths about food. The rest of the time she reads Robin McKinley and Lois McMaster Bujold, plays boardgames like Settlers of Catan, *rears her twins, and writes stories set in her troll-infested North-lands.*

Look for her novels and novellas at your favorite bookstore – online or on Main Street.

J.M. Ney-Grimm maintains a blog featuring flash fiction from her North-lands and other tidbits unearthed by her ever-active curiosity.

Visit her at JMNey-Grimm.com.